PRAISE FOR
COME WITH THE FIRE

"Immediately grabs your attention and makes the reader want to find out what's going on. I adore how well it ties in at the end as well, it's brilliant!"
—EMILY WRIGHT, author of *Tamara King*

"A powerful protagonist like Emily is like a wildfire that can barely be contained. She may be quiet, but shy? No; Emily is passionate!"
—BETA READER

"I love strong Black female protagonists —bonus points for being culturally specific because it promises I would learn more about a way of life I may not be familiar with."**—BETA READER**

"The grandmother and father characters were probably my favorites. I love the sense of home they provide. The strong-willed and wise grandmother shows where Emily gets her passion and wit. Her father serves a similar purpose. With him, she can be herself. He shoots straight. Some of the best parts of this story was just describing home life, food, traditions, and ways of thinking and speaking, and those things come primarily through Emily, her father, and grandmother."
—BETA READER

"I liked that the reading was approachable, which makes for a quick and enjoyable read."**—BETA READER**

"I loved reading about Emily's home culture and the little details about what she was wearing and how she did self-care. Those details brought a warmth to the story."
—BETA READER

*A beta reader is a test reader of an unreleased work of literature who gives feedback from the point of view of an average reader. Thanks to Black&Bookish Beta-reader service.

COME WITH THE FIRE

a novel

JULIANNE MUNDLE

MUNDLE BOOKS

MUNDLE BOOKS are registered trademarks of Julianne Mundle
created by Photologo®

(Paperback) This publication has been assigned: 978-1-7778983-0-4
(Ebook) This publication has been assigned: 978-1-7778983-1-1

Subjects include Fiction
Content Warning: Racism, Bullying, and Fires

First paperback edition December 2021
Proofread by Ma Elena A.
Edited by Brittany Chung Campbell

Book design and illustrated by Dominique Jones
Fonts used from Adobe Fonts /Typekit

To my beloved homeland, Jamaica.

Love always.

TABLE OF CONTENTS

PATOIS GALLEY

Affi: have to

Arite: Alright

Cyaan: can't

Dats: that's; that is.

Gi weh: give away

Guh/Gaa: go

Gwaan: go on

likkle: little

Mi nuh love dat: I don't love that

Nuh: Don't

Oh Zeen: oh cool

Ole: old

Yu: you

Weh: What/Where

Wid: with

Weh you deh: Where are you?

Wah gwaan?: What's happening?/ How are you?

Unnu: you (plural)

PROLOGUE

Autumn, 2016. Toronto, Canada.

When the one you trust betrays you, you have two options:
Forgive the yout, walk away and never look back or bun down di place and
watch it all burn.

A heavy laugh bubbled up and seeped out of my mouth as I bent over my journal, frantically writing my thoughts before they disappeared again. After everything that happened within the past few weeks, I could only laugh and write about the current state of my life. At least it made for good material. Resting my back against the cross rail of the cold metal chair, I crossed my arms around my body, still shuddering from the thick scent of smoke clinging to my coily hair. To the cop sitting in front of me and my mom pacing back and forth behind her, I probably looked and sounded hysterical . . . but what else was new these days?

"Emily!" Mom's voice sounded more like a threat to shut the hell up.

"Miss Morrison, put the notebook away now. Are you ready to speak?" The female police officer asked.

My eyes stayed low, only looking at the chipped red nail polish left on the tip of my pointer finger. Then I noticed the cop moving closer to me, pulling out a chair and taking a seat across the table. Now a huge metal boundary separated us from the truth.

Reaching for her paper cup of room temperature coffee, chilling near the edge of the table, she took a swig and continued. "Emily, if you know something, you need to say something . . . you're not in the best situation right now."

Click-Click-Click! My attention shot to my mother's slingbacks, distracting me. She was tapping aggressively on the gray ceramic tiles that covered the floor.

I hate those silver pumps. My mom's shoe collection is so lit, yet she wore these, today. Okay, Emily, focus. Every tap of those ugly slingbacks urged me to speak. I took a deep breath and leaned back further into my seat. Words crawled up my throat and banged, with their fists, on my lips, trying to come out. But I swallowed them back into the pit of my stomach . . . silencing them. Now, I could feel the cop's eyes staring into my soul, but I dared myself not to meet her gaze.

"Emily, if you did this, we need to know. You could've hurt many people today." The cop said in a firm tone.

"W-what do you want me to say?" I snapped back. Internally, I kissed my teeth. *Someone probably already convinced her everything that happened was my fault . . . It was always my fault.*

While I could control my words, my tears were rebellious. Hot tears escaped from my eyes and ran down my face. I looked up at the ceiling and begged them to stop flowing. It stopped, and I continued. "Although I'd like to take credit for setting the fire, I swear to God, it wasn't me. If I've learned one thing about that uppity private high school it's this: you never know who's wearing a mask and who is genuine."

"Emily, just talk to the woman and tell her the truth!" My mother stomped her foot. The sound from the heel of her shoe meeting the ceramic, echoed in the silence.

If the cop wasn't here, my mother would have flown across the table and shook me until the truth fell out. She was afraid for me and I knew this could ruin my future, but the only thing I could think about right now was him. Thinking about him broke me all over again, and I felt the tears creeping back up, but I wiped them away before they could fall. It made little sense to shed tears over him now.

Numb, I glanced at my mother's face one more time, her eyes signaling for me to tell the truth. Resting my elbow on the metal table, I placed my chin on the palm of my hand and continued stalling. "You're probably wondering how this even happened. I've asked myself the question a bunch of times in the past few weeks." My voice trembled as I spoke. *Not again.* By now, I had oppressed my tears enough. They were free and streaming down my cheeks.

The cop reached across the table and placed a tissue in my hand. Her touch startled me, and I looked up to meet her eyes. Our skin tone was so similar, our hands almost melted into each other. She looked at me as if she understood. She actually wanted to listen to what I had to say. My defenses suddenly wilted like a dying rose. This was exhausting, and they knew it. With a dramatic exhale and the falling of my shoulders, I signaled I was ready to speak. The cop motioned to my mother to leave the room, and two other men escorted her to the coffee machine.

"I don't know where to start," I said in almost a whisper.

"Every story has a beginning, so maybe we should start from there."

CHAPTER 1

OH, HOLY TRINITY

The annual Girl's Day assembly at Trinity Collegiate featured Toronto's most established female TV icons. It was the one day a year women took over the entire downtown campus. The boys had a non-instructional day and stayed home . . . I envied them. On Girl's Day, the faculty transformed our theatre auditorium into a pink, giggle-fest of teenage girls delicately clapping for the panel of blonde TV personalities on stage. My eyes panned across the long white table. On this panel of female empowerment was every Canadian blonde bombshell we all watched nationwide, at home in our living rooms with our parents.

"In conclusion, young ladies, you are strong and if you remember to just breathe, no one can make you feel inferior." The guest speaker's broadcaster voice belted out into the auditorium. It was a high school assembly, but her speech sounded more like a presidential address to her constituents.

Just breathe, I thought to myself. *As if deep breathing would help me battle my inner and outer demons at Trinity.*

A roaring of delicate hands clapped. Everyone's hands fluttered at the pace of hummingbirds. *They even clapped the same here.* More hummingbird claps filled the auditorium as Caroline Cooke's speech concluded. When the clapping turned into a fierce standing ovation, I stayed seated. I was unmoved by the generic speech about her legendary career as Toronto's main anchorwoman. Just like the year before, Girl's Day wasn't for girls like me. Girls like me weren't even a part of the conversation.

Two sophomore girls bobbed up and down to the music blaring from the speakers, I squeezed between them, snapped a photo of the panel, and tweeted my frustration.

Ding! The tweet travelled out to my 500 followers, mostly strangers and childhood friends back home in Jamaica, who liked my dry sense of humour and random thinking tangents. *At least, I think they did.*

When Caroline Cooke finally took a breath from talking, Principal Kowalski slipped in to address the audience. Kowalski was a tall, thin, plain-looking woman with long, mousy brown hair wrapped into a tight bun at the nape.

"Okay ladies, let's give it up for our panel of experts!" Principal Kowalski screamed into the microphone. Her Polish accent echoed and bounced off the walls.

"Woot! Woot!" a tall redhead senior chanted over my shoulder.

Being a sophomore in a predominantly white school is hard enough, but listening to an annual speech about "female empowerment" that didn't address actual issues in other communities of women was truly more than I could take today.

"It's time for women to join forces, come together and take on the world!" Caroline's acoustical voice echoed throughout the room even without the microphone in her hand.

"I hate assemblies," I mumbled under my breath. It's like forced programming for the mind. They haul us out of class and make us sit in specific order. You can't sit with friends or even try to sit in another homeroom. On this day, the stars aligned only to punish me. I got the luxury of sitting beside the classmate I couldn't stand the most . . . Katherine Caldwell. Slouched and sinking into the red fabric chair, I kissed my teeth for the thousandth time.

"Shhh," Katherine hissed, aggressively directing it towards me. Her blue eyes were their own source of light in the dark auditorium. Now they were piercing into me, the way a mother silences their child without having to say a word.

Did this girl just shhh me?

We weren't friends in the slightest, but Katherine always seemed to be interested in me. No matter how many times I dryly told her, "I don't care for you."

"Can you stop policing my behaviour?" I snapped at her, giving her my fiercest side glare. *She just loves to nuff up herself all in my space.*

When I first enrolled at Trinity, I didn't know why this tiny blonde creature roamed the halls as if she owned the place. Until I found out weeks later, her family *literally* owned a wing of the school. The Caldwells donated tons of money to Trinity Collegiate. Her father was a notable financial guy for the city's hockey team. Her mother was a TV network executive . . . and not to mention best friends with Caroline Cooke. Both of her siblings went through the Trinity legacy, too. Known for her high achieving grades and athletic skills, Katherine's primary goal was to outperform and overachieve at all times. When she finally lost interest in my antics and shot her attention back to the stage, her shortened plaid skirt swayed as she clapped the tips of her fingers in excitement. With perfect posture, she stood on the tips of her toes so everyone could see her golden hair above the crowd.

"Loser . . ." her best friend and sidekick spat out in my direction.

I ignored the taunting and focused my attention on the exit door. Yes, man, this is a terrific morning, I thought.

As the room slowly dispersed, a long line of students formed in front of Caroline as she signed copies of her new book entitled, *Woman's Worth: We are Strong; We are Brave and We Can Accomplish Anything.*

Passing the lineup of girls, I studied the energy of the room. For everyone who looked like Caroline, it was a joyous occasion and a chance to network for summer internships and mentors. Meanwhile, I was extremely uncomfortable and just wanted to go home. When I searched the faces of the girls who were close to me, I was confident that I was the only one feeling excluded.

How could a school that prides itself on its progressive culture, not cater to diversity and inclusion?

In a slow procession out of the auditorium, Caroline's voice echoed after me. "Women have faced many barriers, yes, but often we create our own. We don't apply for that job because we assume that we will not get it . . . that is self-sabotage!"

How did this woman get the mic back?

I rolled my eyes, squirming past masses of teenage girls waiting for a chance to speak to Caroline. Walking out of the auditorium in the opposite direction was like walking out of the Air Canada Centre after a Drake concert.

Her voice echoed again. "Women are powerful, and we have the same opportunities as men. We need to latch on to them!" The sound of applause and cheers erupted behind me as I pushed through the heavy auditorium doors . . . and then suddenly I saw the light.

Entering the stone and marble halls of Trinity, the floor to ceiling glass windows greeted me with the warm sun. I inhaled the silence, waiting for my eyes to adjust when more girls came rushing out behind me. Closely packed, bumping into my body and then scattering in all directions, filling the grand hall of the school.

I felt my phone vibrate in the back pocket of my uniform pants, took it out and looked at my Twitter notifications:

Marsha Henry
@MzPetiteJA

Damn, it's like that up in the great old north, eh lol?

3:00 · 2016 · Twitter Web App

96 Retweets   **88** Quote Tweets   **153** Likes

Lisa Jenkins
@LadyKane

Are tall blonde ladies the only girls in Toronto?

3:00 · 2016 · Twitter Web App

10 Retweets   **1** Quote Tweets   **10** Likes

Ding! My tweet got 15 shares and a few comments rolled in.

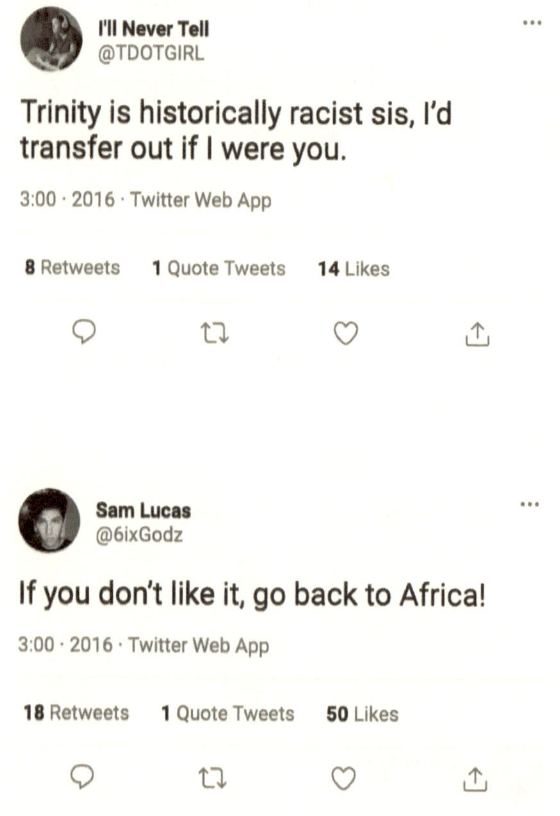

When the trolls comment, that's when you know it's time to put down the phone. I placed my phone in my pocket when I felt a bony shoulder crash into mine. Clinging to a freshly signed copy of Caroline's book, Katherine brushed by me and shot a dirty glance my way. I commended her for her "discreet" attempt, but I definitely saw it. That was the thing about

Trinity, people seemed to turn into trolls when no one was looking, but at school, everyone pretended to get along . . . or something like it.

"That was a great assembly, don't you think?" Katherine called out to me. She was walking backwards to face me and waving Caroline's book in the air.

That was a great assembly, don't you think? I mimicked it in my head and walked after her. "I'm sure it was for you, Katherine, but personally I would've liked to see more representation." I calmly retorted, speeding up so she could hear me.

Katherine's wide blue eyes dramatically rolled back into her head. "Everything is not about race, Emily. Gosh, you're so annoying to talk to sometimes," she sounded irritated.

I passed her, walking further down the hall heading to my locker. "Then don't talk to me," I said over my shoulder. "Everything is not about race for you, Katherine, because it doesn't have to be." My Jamaican accent was stronger than ever.

I walked away briskly toward my locker and left her standing there talking to herself. The heels from my suede, black, chunky pumps echoed as I walked through the matrix, the longest hallway in school. This long, dark alley led to classes and teachers who pledged to teach us the truth but hid the actual truth somewhere else. *Kudos to the clever intellectual who named that part of the school.*

There, in the matrix at Trinity Collegiate, were endless Canadian History banners and memorabilia. An alumnus interviewed former Prime Minister Brian Mulroney, and so a shadow box displayed the newspaper article and photos. They plastered inspirational quotes from figures like William Lyon Mackenzie King and William Churchill in big, black, bold, italicised letters across the walls. But there was no posting about Indigenous communities or Viola Desmond, the Canadian civil rights activist or Rosemary Brown, who was the first black Canadian woman elected to a Canadian provincial legislature. There wasn't one newspaper clipping with interviews from Michael-Lee Chin or Donald Oliver, the Jamaican-Canadian business executive or the first black Canadian to have a seat in the senate. This reminded me of one thing every single day, there was absolutely nothing here to make myself or any other student of colour believe that they could be successful . . . but I was used to that by now.

I got to my locker and put in the combination. The grey, metal door squeaked as it opened and revealed a portal to my personal haven. The metal door hung by a thread and the locker was all rusty, but inside were all my favourite things. On a broken hook in the back of my locker was a letter I placed in a small brown picture frame, reading:

Home is always in your heart. Wherever you are, home is. Remember your talent, remember your voice, remember who you are.

Love Mrs. Johnson

By now, the letter was tattered and worn but I read it for motivation so many times. Now it hung there in my locker, behind the dented metal door, among Polaroids of friends from back home.

"If you have trouble fitting in, post this up somewhere you can see, every day." My favourite English teacher, told me. She not only taught me how to write, but she taught me the importance of self-worth.

I've lived in Canada for three years and it hasn't felt like home. The transition was tough, yet I always kept waiting for it to get better. Now, my accent comes and goes and my friends have their own lives that don't include me. I looked at the letter and wished I was back home among the coconut trees. *Living in Jamaica would be different for me at this point. What do you do when you are too Jamaican for Canada and too Canadian for Jamaica?*

CHAPTER 2

THE ORACLE'S ALWAYS WATCHING

The schools in Toronto looked like museums and students sat on grand stone staircases eating their lunch, like on Gossip Girl. I remember when I first stepped into this building. Trinity made me feel a bit of excitement, but that excitement quickly faded when the reflection of mom's Mac Ruby Woo lipstick appeared in the office secretary's prescription glasses as they argued.

"Jamaica is an English-speaking country. What do you mean she has to take ESL?" Mom stood astute in pumps that accentuated her knee-length nude wrap dress. Her jet black curls bounced as she nodded her head in agreement with the words leaving her mouth.

Sitting on one of two plastic seats provided for visitors, my knees locked, skinny ankles crossed, and my sweaty hands clasped together in my lap. My hair was slick in a bun and I wore a black cotton skater dress with sheer, full-length tights. My ballet flats danced as I shook my feet under the chair, watching the exchange go down. With bated breath, I wondered if maybe I should've listened to my mom and worn my black church pumps instead.

"I'm sorry, lady, but that is our policy. Newcomers to Canada must take English as a Second Language course before English at the academic level."

This was the eighth school we visited to decide where my academic future would land. A co-worker told my mother about a luxury catholic private school that was encouraging "diverse students" to apply for academic scholarships . . . I qualified. By the time we got to this school, my father stayed in the car. He didn't see the point of having several school tours when the curriculum was all the same. On the way to this last school, he ranted about it the entire drive. "This whole 'diversity thing' calling for students of colour, only tells me one thing," my dad clicked his tongue before continuing. "They probably need to meet a diversity quota or something."

My mother ignored him and applied another layer of Ruby Woo. "According to the brochure, Trinity Collegiate is a *private institution*, ranging from pre-kindergarten to grade 12," my mother regurgitated back as she read the pamphlet in the car.

"Oh cool," I said sarcastically.

Now I was sitting in the office, and I was over it. I just wanted to pick a school so we could go home. I didn't care which one. They all gave me the same vibe; uppity, uniformed, and non-Jamaican. My old school was on par, if not superior to Trinity. For one, my high school motto definitely trumped Trinity's: "Momento Audere Semper" which meant "Remember, always be bold". It resonated more with me than "Burning with the zeal for truth," but I mean, go off, Trinity. Now in the office, I read the words engraved into the stone plaque on the wall, "Flagrans Veritatis Studio."

"This is ridiculous..." my mom uttered under her breath."

"Then maybe you should go somewhere better suited." The lady in glasses returned to her desk, dismissing our presence and typing aggressively.

"My daughter is the top of her class in Clarendon."

"Clarendon?" The woman replied, "Well, this is Canada, lady."

Mom sighed. She was so excited about putting me in a fancy school that she didn't expect to be greeted with hostility and hesitation. She didn't need to say it, but I knew she wanted to avoid the "angry black woman" stereotype. Too late... you show any form of displeasure and they instantly classify you as the angry black woman.

Listening to my mother and the lady go back and forth while I sat quietly was as foreign as this country was to me. She would've never been so passive if we were back home. Then again, I couldn't recall a time when we faced discrimination like this back home.

"I am sure there is an assessment she can take to prove her eligibility," my mom urged. She was referring to the fact that I had to take standardized exams to be accepted to my high school in Jamaica.

A few moments later, a colleague of the lady appeared from behind the door marked "Staff Only." She was slender and her reddish-orange lipstick was way over lined around her thin lips. Her auburn hair hung loosely in the messiest messy bun I'd ever seen. She approached us slowly, standing in solidarity with the lady wearing glasses.

"Your daughter may take a 30 minute English and Math Assessment, but I must warn you it will be rigorous and extremely challenging. Most newcomers don't make it through half of each test," the auburn-haired lady said.

"So now she has to take a math test too . . . are you people serious?" Mom blurted out. I think it's safe to say that if you'd cut her arm, you would have seen no blood at that point.

"Mom, it's fine. I'll do it," I said sheepishly. I followed the lady behind the "Staff Only" door.

She pointed to a desk and chair at the far end of the room, directing me with a waving gesture. "Please sit there."

I obeyed.

Giving me a fake smile, she handed me the English test first. "You have 30 minutes, after which I will take the paper from you." She said, sliding the test across the desk towards me.

I tapped my pencil, while my feet did their dancing bit again. Obviously sensing my nervousness, an unattractive smirk suddenly plastered across the woman's face, highlighting cracks in her cakey foundation.

I turned the paper over and looked at the first question in awe. "Excuse me, are you sure this is the right paper?" I winced at how foreign I sounded.

I hated my accent at that very moment. It made me stick out like a sore thumb.

"I am positive, sweetie, see I told you it's a grueling test." She moaned from the desk she sat behind.

I took my gaze away from her and looked down at the paper again.

Fill in the blanks with the correct homophone:
"Jack and Jill [blew/blue] the petals off the flowers."

Did they know I was going into grade seven and not four? I read each question slowly and filled in the answers. This had to be some sort of trick. There was no way this was the actual test. She was setting me up or something. . . . I wasn't sure. After eighteen minutes, I let her know I finished with a raised hand.

She said nothing to me and handed me the Math test.

Answer this story problem:
"If John has five marbles and gives Mary four marbles, how many marbles does John have left?"

My eyes fixated on the question. Nooo, a must joke dis, I thought. I completed the test in twenty minutes, handed the paper to her, and walked out of the room.

My mom was sitting in the waiting area, tapping her feet and glaring at the lady in glasses. As the lady sat at her desk, the tapping from her keyboard echoed throughout the silent room.

"You're done already?" Mom asked me.

I nodded.

"When and how will we get the results?" My mom asked impatiently, clutching her black YSL tote handbag.

"You can wait for them if you would like to." The lady answered.

"I'd love to," my mom challenged.

"Perfect! It shouldn't be too long." The lady smiled and headed to another room.

We waited outside of the receptionist's office.

"How was it?" My mom berated me.

I shrugged.

"What do you mean, you don't know? You better make sure you don't fail it. It will just give them one more reason to judge us."

I said nothing.

Ten minutes later, the auburn-haired lady came looking for us in the hallway with a huge grin on her face, revealing even more cracks in her cakey foundation. "Honey, congratulations! You got 100 percent on both tests!"

In an instant, I went from being an immigrant who couldn't speak English to a star student . . . in her eyes. My mom took the test papers from her and looked at the questions. She looked at me quizzically.

I shrugged and chuckled.

"Okay, let's get the heck out of here," she said.

Before we could make it for the exit, the lady with glasses burst out of the office doors, chasing after us in heels. "Oh, Madam, before you go, here is your welcome package!" She ran down the hall, waving a large yellow packet at us. "Here is your class information, where to buy her uniform, what church most of the families attend, and a parent contact list for your reference."

"Why do we need all of this?" my mom interrupted. She looked excited and puzzled at the same time.

"Well, Trinity is also a network of affluent families. We all help each other out. Our kids go to the same school, so we might as well be friends, right?" The lady said, using her manicured hands to talk. She directed her attention to me next. "Honey, you're going to be assigned to Katherine Caldwell, she's your welcome buddy, she'll teach you the ropes of this place, okay?" Then she looked back at my mother. "Katherine's parents' numbers are on the back of that list."

My mother nodded her head. We were both stunned at the switch in her behaviour. As we walked down the long hallway towards the exit of the school, I looked up at my mother. "Did we just join a cult?" I whispered to her.

Growing up in Jamaica, I didn't have to fight to prove myself. But at that moment, when my accent made me feel inferior, I made a vow to always be proud of my island accent and show up at Trinity with confidence, even though being ostracized and uncomfortable was constant here. It's been three years now, and no matter how hard I try, I still feel like the little girl in ballet flats, so nervous that her feet still dance under her chair.

***

Ding, Ding! Twitter notifications interrupted my reminiscing, and I looked down at my phone.

TDOTGIRL and 3 others started following you.

I kept scrolling down my feed as I closed my locker. Closing it was like detonating a bomb. The lock was so finicky I stopped to cautiously turn the dial to the exact number, making it close firmly. My locker was old, broken, and rusty. It seemed as if I was so invisible that after asking the office to fix my locker or give me a new one, they totally disregarded me.

Ding, Ding, Ding! More notifications appeared on the screen.

Hailey Thomas
@Blondesundoll

Caroline Cooke is the epitome of
modern feminism, loser

4:00 · 2016 · Twitter Web App

20 Retweets   **4** Quote Tweets   **60** Likes

Marshall Ellis
@KingstonYute

You girl's day soun' lame still, hurry and
come back home Em

4:00 · 2016 · Twitter Web App

20 Retweets   **4** Quote Tweets   **60** Likes

Francis Porter
@FKPorter

I see you, try smiling, why don't cha!

4:00 · 2016 · Twitter Web App

3 Retweets   **9** Quote Tweets   **10** Likes

What the hell?! Where is he? I shot around to look for any sign of him. I looked over my shoulders in both directions. The halls were clearing out now and everyone was heading to their sports cars out in the parking lot. In an instant, I was completely alone in the matrix. No one was there, so I ignored the tweet and kept walking down the hall towards the city bus stop.

At the end of the matrix, I passed by a group of girls and a football player on their phones. They were gossiping about nothing and everything. Derek came up to me and started walking at my pace.

I rolled my eyes, "I thought they banned jocks today." I said in passing, annoyed by his presence.

"Wah g'waan sweet bits." He yelled in my ear, although he was right beside me. Derek was a bi-racial football player who often bugged me whenever he saw me.

"What," I said as I kept walking, keeping my head straight. My eyes squinted together in disgust. I knew of Derek as "the token black linebacker" and I was not interested in getting to know him personally. The entire school knew him well. He had really greasy cornrows. It was as if he bathed in Blue Magic. He rolled the sleeves of his golf shirt to his shoulders, revealing very undeveloped bicep and tricep muscles. The aroma of axe body spray threatened my nostrils, forcing me to stifle a sneeze.

"We should chill sometime," he said.

"I'm chilling quite fine by myself." I quickened my pace and left him behind. I could faintly hear him mumbling something about bitches, and I had no time for his toxic masculinity.

"If you lighten up, people would actually like you!" he screamed behind me.

His remark didn't faze me. I was used to it by now. The difference between him and me was he conformed to fit in, I didn't. I wouldn't shuck and jive for these entitled kids, and I knew for sure I would not find my husband in high school.

Right beside the school entrance was the newspaper room. I placed a hand on the door handle while glancing into the office, as I always did each day. I noticed Katherine and a group of girls from the newspaper chilling inside the office. Her silky straight hair flowed with the breeze blowing in from the ajar door. The ladies laughed as they discussed where they wanted to eat dinner that night. Truthfully, I wanted to be a part of the Oracle newspaper team. It was one of the most renowned high school newspapers in Toronto. But apart from me not wanting to end up writing gossip news about celebrity entertainment, as the other students did, I doubted they would accept my work. I anxiously thought about submitting a perfect piece about acknowledging systemic racism in Canadian society, only to have it ripped apart and judged.

Finally, I exited the hallowed halls of "little Hogwarts" as I frequently described it in my head, and arrived at the bus stop. I moved my headphones from around my neck and put them over my ears. "Rock Away" by Beres Hammond soothed my nerves as I played my roots reggae playlist. I kept the volume low so I could watch my surroundings.

DING! I looked down at my phone to see a random tweet.

Before I could even spin around, I heard, "Em!" over my music. I turned around and finally saw my stalker . . . it was just Francis.

"So what, did you change your Twitter handle today?" I said, turning to give him my usual one-arm hug.

"Yea, FKPorter sounds like a legit journalist handle, eh?" He retorted, pinching my cheek with his fingers.

I rolled my eyes. "So what does the 'k' stand for?" I asked.

"King, duh!"

We both laughed.

Francis was such an enigma. He was just shy of 6 feet and was what my grandmother called "strapping," which meant he was a muscular, thick, sturdy young man. Anyone's first impression of him would be that he was a serious athlete. He used to be a star athlete but I knew him as a sensitive poet who enjoyed debating world issues. Francis and I met in grade seven when he sat beside the "new girl" in class, and we've been "batty and bench" ever since. We clicked right off the bat. I guess we both felt like outsiders. Of course, he fit in more than I did because he basically grew up with most of the kids. But he was the former jock who enjoyed reciting scenes from "Macbeth" in the cafeteria, and I was the pro-Black, weirdo, Jamaican girl who encouraged him to write. We were known . . . not for the right reasons, but we had no problem with that. People seemed to think that Francis and I were involved romantically, but this couldn't be further from the truth. I always shut those accusations down.

"What are you doing here?" I asked, not surprised that Francis would be on school property on a day he wasn't supposed to.

"Oh! I came to grab my gear from my locker. There's a fire on Bloor Street again, it's like the second arson this month, and I'm covering it for my submission for the Oracle. I think there's a story there." He replied as he grabbed me and hugged me with a wide grin.

"Get off!" I laughed pushing him away. "What's with all the fires this summer?"

"No clue, but there's a trend going on. All the buildings being burnt down are Toronto housing . . . a coincidence? I think not!"

Every year, the school paper takes submissions from students who want to get on the newspaper team. The assignment? Find a good story, write a good article, then submit it.

"Dude, get on your submission!" Francis said as he danced around me on the sidewalk. I laughed and tried to push him, but he kept dodging my advances. Just then, Katherine came walking through the school doors, with minions behind her. She looked at us, stopped for a bit, and kept walking.

"I can't stand her." I winced. Luckily, she made a right turn and continued whichever journey she was on. When she was out of sight, I turned back to Francis. "So can I come?" I laughed, raising my right eyebrow.

"Okay, sure, but is your mom going to have a cow?" He said, flaring his nostrils and opening his eyes wide, imitating my mother's angry face.

"Rude and racist!" I warned, elbowing him in the gut.

"Ow! I was joking, eh?" He laughed and held his torso at the same time.

"So how long have you been here and how much of that woman's dumb speech did you hear?" I asked.

"Enough to know that you're about to lead us to a deep debate on white privilege and how much you can't stand white people," he laughed.

"First . . ." I said in a very stern tone.

"Here we go," he said, rolling his light brown eyes and laughing.

"No, there's no here we go. First, I don't hate white people, and please don't say that as we stand here on a white man's sidewalk." I looked over my shoulder, making sure no one heard Francis' remark.

"You literally just contradicted yourself, Em." He said in a serious tone, as if he had made some sort of point.

I looked at him. "Elaborate," I said as the bus approached us slowly, coming to a halt.

"Okay, you said you don't hate 'those people', and in that same sentence you said that we're standing on 'their' sidewalk."

I tapped my presto card on the automated fare machine before entering the bus. As I made my way slowly inside, I shot Francis a look of annoyance. He always incorporates air quotes in a conversation simply because it makes him feel smarter.

"What? You know that 'their sidewalk' is simply a metaphor, right? I'm just saying that the leaders of the country are primarily white and I don't need people thinking I hate white people. Is that an incorrect statement?" I asked. I could tell this was going to be like our usual racial debates where I make actual points and he brushes them off.

"No, it isn't an incorrect statement," he said, imitating my tone. "I just think that it's very pointed. Should you penalize white people because they are leaders of the country?"

Walking down the aisle, we found seats near the back. My tight 4b shoulder-length curls wrapped around each other and brushed against the beads of sweat running down the back of my neck. I gathered it all with two hands and formed it into the usual messy crown that sat on top of my head. It was early autumn now, and it was 24 degrees Celsius, but it felt like 40 with the howling humidity.

"You're missing my point, as per usual," I replied stiffly. "Francis, let me explain something to you for the umpteenth time," I began, full Jamaican mode activated. "I do not, have never, and will never hate a person because of their race." I was gesturing a bit too much with my hands. "That does not mean that I am blind to the fact that certain people are more privileged than others. What I cannot respect is people ignoring their privilege and pretending as if racialized communities, especially Black & Indigenous people, are treated equally in society . . . and that, fam, is exactly what happened in that presentation with Caroline Cooke today."

Francis looked around at onlookers tuning into our conversation. As my voice grew more stern, he squirmed in his seat.

"And to answer the second part of your argument," I continued. "I am not saying that we should penalize white people, but they should not be the only leaders of this country. Are you telling me that in 2016 it's okay for there to be no diversity in leadership?"

"Okay, let's table this conversation for now, eh." He said dismissively, waving his right palm in my face. "This is probably too heavy a discussion for public transit."

I rolled my eyes. This was his typical Canadian response to conflict. I turned to face the window. Lately, there seemed to be a shift in our friendship. Most of the time, we got along fine. But talking to Francis was becoming increasingly difficult, and I often wondered if we were just on the cusp of growing apart.

When the bus stopped at the intersection of Bloor and Ossington, we could see crowds of people. Everyone looked distraught and clustered on either side of the street. Throughout the summer, these fires had become a social spectacle. They were happening almost weekly now, and it made the news every single time. Out of the front windshield of the bus, I could see cop cars blocking the roads off with orange cones and caution tape. A few blocks away, an old high-rise was engulfed with flames while firefighters rushed into action. Crime in Toronto seemed to ignite every summer, but this time it seemed to continue into autumn. While the rumors said the fires were related to gang violence, others seemed to think there was more to this story, including Francis.

"Alright, from here you can take the subway or the shuttle bus through the back roads, but you gotta get the hell off my bus!" The TTC driver hollered to a lady pestering him for answers.

"Let's go, this is where we get the action," Francis said, jumping off the bus and gunning through the crowds, heading toward the flaming high rise.

"Yea, no worries, don't wait for me," I mumbled to myself as the star journalist student scrummed with local city news officials.

Francis had no fear. He was pretty well connected. His mom was rich and although his father didn't live with him, his dad came from a wealthy family, too. I watched him in action, his agile ability to squeeze into places and just belong. It was so easy for him. Jealousy coursed through me, anger quickly followed. Francis was my best friend, but every time I felt like I had a day of rejection, I would look at him just being himself, and totally feel discouraged in my abilities. It suddenly occurred to me, *what the hell was I even doing here?* Walking off the bus and into the crowds, all I could see was chaos. Angry commuters in grey business attire funneled into the subway, while crowds of onlookers pulled out their phones, taking pictures of the high-rise in flames.

"Get off the bus!" the bus driver yelled at a bunch of teens with their headphones on.

Around me, a few businesses were letting in displaced residents and serving them water. Onlookers watched the fire through their phones and huddled on sidewalks. The building was ablaze with flames and debris, violently scorching each unit one by one. Glass from a broken window fell from the seventh floor and shattered on the cement sidewalk, while Firefighters ran in and out of the building with hoses combating the blaze. On the other end of the barrier, police cars hustled to control the media trucks and public taking photos, trying to get close to the action.

What is it about danger and chaos that makes people go crazy? I thought to myself.

Francis disappeared into the crowd. While everyone watched the flames melt the apartment building, I watched the surrounding people. To the left of me was an alley next to a pizzeria food truck. I had eaten nothing all day, and this sight was making me anxious. I walked toward Bruno's Big Slice, hoping to grab a drink and a veggie slice before meeting up with Francis again.

"Can I have a garden slice and a coke please?"

"Coming right up, sweet heart," the large man took a warm slice from his pizza oven.

"What's with all the fires in this neighbourhood?" I asked.

Bruno emerged from the cooler with a chilled can of coke in his grasp. "Oh come on, you don't know?" He placed my food on the counter before accepting my ten dollar bill. "These high-rise developers are pissed that the city is making their buildings into community housing. So what do they do to the immigrants and the poor guys like us? They get rid of our homes, like cockroaches . . . *by accident.*" He placed three toonies in the palm of my hand. "Here's your change."

"By accident?" I said, confused.

"Oh yea, if it's an 'accidental fire' these rich guys get a bunch of insurance money to build new buildings. While most of us are out here left on our asses."

I slipped the money in my pocket and took a huge bite of pizza. "Thanks," I said before heading into the alleyway to find somewhere to sit and eat. But when I walked past the alley, I saw a woman. Crouched down and leaning against a brick wall, she hugged a little girl and boy close to her chest. I watched her as she watched the flames melt the structure of the high-rise apartment building. When I looked around, no one seemed to notice her but me. She was invisible to the bystanders who were live-tweeting the events of the fire, but I saw her and we made eye contact. Her face imprinted into my memory and before my mind could process what I was doing, I was already inches from the woman and children. Covered in soot, she wore a tattered grey sweatsuit and no shoes. She was shaking and her eyes looked at me wildly.

"I don't want to bother you, I just want to help." I approached her slowly. "Once, when I was a child, I witnessed a robbery at a small treat shop on my way home from school. It left me paralyzed in fear." I drawled on anxiously. I knew she wasn't listening to me, but I knew what it was like to witness something traumatic. I wanted to make sure she was alright, but her expression shot needles through my heart. She was terrified, and no one even noticed she was there. I looked around for a paramedic. "Excuse me, a woman and two children need medical attention here!" I screamed out into the crowd.

"No!" she shrieked and grabbed the children running down the alley. I followed.

"Miss, wait!" I took off after her and followed her down an adjacent alleyway full of graffiti. "Miss, I just want to help, please let me get you somewhere to sleep."

The lady stopped and looked over her shoulder, "We're fine, we can head to the shelter ourselves."

I approached her slowly once more. "I could get you guys a room, at least for the night . . . at a hotel." I focused my attention on the children next. "What about something to eat and a clean place to take a bath?" I didn't know where this good samaritan spirit came from, but there was something about this woman that felt so familiar.

"You're a child, I'm not taking anything from you." She said she wasn't looking back at me anymore. I could hear a faint accent, but her voice was trembling. It was hard to pinpoint which island she was from. "I can help, it's not that much, really." I insisted and watched as the tension moved from the woman's shoulders and down her body.

Ding! I grabbed my phone out of my pocket and glanced at a tweet from Francis.

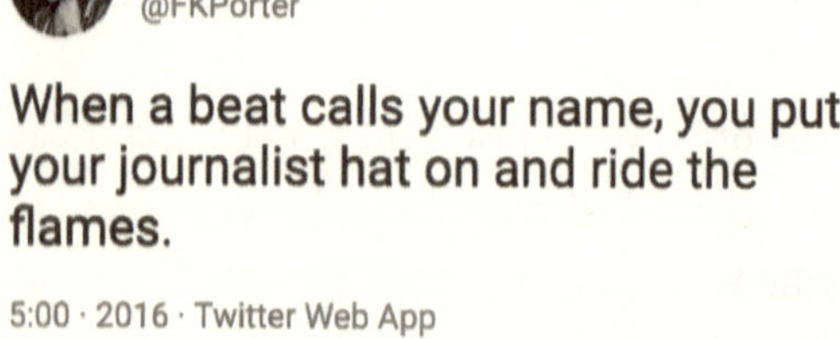

That was the caption accompanying a photo of the apartment building wrapped in fire. Good to know Francis was alright, I guess, great to know he didn't give two shits about where I was. I put the phone back into the back pocket of my pants and continued speaking to the woman.

"Listen, I don't know you or where you're going to end up tonight, it's my guess the shelters will be full and uncomfortable . . . let me take you to the nearest hotel so you can at least have somewhere comfortable to stay."

Her eyes pierced through my flesh. She studied my expression, and I remained stoic, even though I wanted to cry. I wasn't sure why, but something about this woman reminded me of home.

Soon, the four of us sat in a quadrant of the streetcar in total silence. I knew the nearest Holiday Inn was a few stops away. "Just a few more stops," I said to the woman. She had said little to me since we got on. It looked as if her entire world collapsed, along with her home in that fire, I didn't feel the need to bug her with conversation.

Next to us, a woman in a power suit looked over and focused on the mother's bare feet. Her French manicured hands folded over her leopard print purse.

"Can I help you?" I asked, my neck rolling like a bobblehead. She looked away quickly and buried her Chanel glasses into a romance novel.

"Thank you." The woman whispered, holding the little girl closer to her chest.

"What's your name?" I said to the boy in the seat next to her. The woman placed a hand firmly on his leg and shook her head. The boy turned away from me to face the window.

"Next stop, Queen Street West." A voice said over the transit speaker.

"We get off here," I mentioned to the woman.

Moments later, I motioned for the mother to have a seat in the lobby while I booked a room with a credit card my parents gave me for emergencies. After a phony story about checking my aunt into a room, they gave us two sets of keys. I handed them both to the woman.

"Thank you." Her eyes still looked hollow.

"No problem," I said.

Taking the keys from me, she grabbed my hands. "I will pay you back. I'm not no homeless woman. I'll find you and pay you back."

Finally, I could pinpoint her accent. "She's Jamaican too," I said to myself.

Then she disappeared into the elevators.

I stood in the hotel lobby, listening to the traffic on the downtown streets. When I heard my phone go off, it brought me back to reality, and I instinctively knew it was him.

Where the hell are you? Meet me at Bathurst. I gotta show you what I got.

I'm not too far, I'm on my way!

***

During the 20-minute bus ride home, Francis talked to himself about the photos he took, the quotes he snagged from interviews, riding with the emergency services to the hospital, and the "bomb" submission he was going to create over the weekend.

"Isn't it illegal to let a kid ride in the back of an ambulance for fun?" I asked, interrupting his grand tale.

"Dude, I ran up there like yea I'm supposed to be here, don't mind me." He stopped when he realized I wasn't listening.

I sat there fidgeting, fighting the urge to curse him out for being self-centered when there were actual families out on the streets tonight. I began talking, whether or not he was listening. "You know, I was walking around near Bruno's while you were playing 'Canadian Anderson Cooper'."

"Yea and . . ." Francis said, scrolling through the photos on his DSLR.

"Well, there was a woman in the alley… it looked like she was homeless because of that fire." He looked over with a quizzical look. Now I got his attention.

"Yea . . . she had no shoes, covered in soot and it was as if the fire blew her entire world up today . . ." My voice trailed off. Why was I so emotional about this?

"Em, you can't take on someone's stuff." Francis placed a hand on my knee and I nudged it off.

"I didn't take on anything. I used my emergency card to get her and her kids a room for the night . . . she barely wanted my help, anyway," I said, wiping away a tear.

Whenever Francis and I took the bus home, we would always come off at his stop, and then he'd walk me home, which was a block away from his. Of course, we both knew the ritual was pretty silly since the bus route also passed my house, but neither of us questioned the tradition we started in grade seven.

"Let's stop by my house first," he said as we walked off the bus. "My mom is making cookies, you need a pick me up."

Anytime anything got heavy, Francis needed a pick me up.

"Alright, but I can't stay long. I am actually exhausted," I said.

The truth was, I wanted to get home before my mother did, to avoid another episode of "my underage daughter is having sex with her best friend." I was also extremely annoyed with him. No, Francis and I were not engaging in sexual activity of any kind, but you try telling that to a Jamaican mother who never listens.

"Francis?" I said, shaking off the nerves to yell at him. "Please stop dismissing stuff that I say to you, okay? Even if it's not important to you, that doesn't give you the right to make me feel like I am overreacting."

"Yo! What the hell are you talking about, Emily?" he asked, his blondish-brown eyebrows raising in confusion.

"What the hell do you mean, what am I talking about?" I said.

I stopped walking. I slightly raised my voice, neck roll, and hand gesture in full effect. "Do not play me, Francis," I said. "You always do this. Do you know that as my friend you should try to understand how I am feeling? As my friend, take the time to think maybe there is some validity to what I am saying instead of brushing me off or pretending as if I am just being unreasonable."

"Em, are you on your period or something?" he laughed as he turned to face me. "What is all of this dramatic behaviour for . . . you need to chill, eh."

"Francis," I said, trying very hard to control my anger. "I am trying to explain to you how insensitive you can be sometimes."

"Just calm down and tell me what I did wrong, Emily. I can't understand what you are saying over the yelling and the neck roll."

My brown eyes locked with his for a quick second, and then we both started laughing. He mimicked my neck roll in his nerdy flagrance and accompanied it with a snap. "So tell me, sis, what's up? Are you still mad about the tiff we had on the bus?" He asked.

"No . . . yes . . . all I'm saying is that you should hear me out. I only say things because I think they need to be said. You should try to see things from my point of view once in a while." I urged.

"That's fair, Em, but what about *my* perspective?" he said as we resumed our walk.

"What do you mean?" I countered.

"You don't really listen to what I have to say either," he said. "I mean, think about it. You're always saying how bad it is that white people are leaders of the country and how white people need to understand their privilege. Sometimes I think you forget I'm white. Some things you say are really offensive, Em. You can't blame me for history."

"Could it be that you're offended because it's the truth and no one else has ever been brave enough to tell you?" I said in basically a whisper, slowly making eye contact with him.

"Whose truth, though? I don't get it. What privilege do I need to understand? Because it seems to me like you are telling me to apologize or feel guilty for being white. I didn't choose to be born white. I am who I am and frankly, I have no problem with who I am."

"I don't want you to apologize for being white, the same way I will not apologize for being black. I love who I am, too. What privilege do you ask? Well, simply put, you and I are not the same. You and I don't have the same opportunities. You're privileged in society, I'm not."

Francis looked away and rubbed his head nervously. I guess trying to figure out what to say without hurting my feelings. "I hear what you're saying," he said, returning to the previous argument. "But honestly, and don't chew my head off for this, I really don't understand why you walk around acting like you've been oppressed all the time. That lady you helped today, she is oppressed. But your parents send you to a private school, for God's sake. So many people would like to be friends with you if you just gave them the chance. Not every white person is out to get you. It's Canada. We live in a multi-cultural society Em, it's time you act like it."

I kept walking and remained silent.

"Let's be real here," he continued, following closely beside me. "You and I have been friends long enough for me to know that you've had no life-altering experiences of oppression."

I continued walking and remained silent.

"Okay, now you're upset and giving me the silent treatment, eh? Not only is this very immature behavior, but it can also come across as narcissistic." He said with a shrug of his broad shoulders.

I stopped in my place and turned around to face him. "I am trying to find the right words so that I don't come across as insolent, but you have completely overstepped all the boundaries I have set in this friendship."

Now it was his turn to stay quiet.

An unintentional smirk greeted my face. "Francis, if I am being honest, I think you are extremely ignorant," I said as calmly as I could. "I have been living in Canada for three years. Yes, you and I have been friends for three years, close friends in fact. I confide in you about a lot of things and clearly, that has provided you with the ammunition to speak about my life with extreme arrogance. Rest assured, fam, that there are experiences I've faced here in Canada that I have deliberately chosen to omit from our daily conversations out of fear that it would make our friendship awkward. Or out of exhaustion for not wanting to relive the situation. Don't presume to know everything about my life or myself. You know what I allow you to know."

"K," he said after about a silent minute. I ignored his passive tone.

A few more minutes passed and then he spoke up, "Let's just agree to disagree Em, I'm tired of talking about this."

"Fine," I replied.

Leave it to Francis to "agree to disagree".

CHAPTER 3

LIFE IN HILLEL GARDENS

When we approached Francis' grand brownstone entryway, he unlocked his front door by punching in the security code. He always covered the keypad with his other hand, and it amused me as he tried to hide it.

I literally know every crevice and corner of this house by now . . . even his easy-to-guess, four-digit passcode. I shook my head and laughed under my breath.

Hillel Gardens was like one of those neighbourhoods you see on television. Quiet, affluent and gated . . . with very strict rules. As Francis' mom explained to me once, "If you have people coming over to visit, there is no reason they should gather outside on the front lawn. If you don't want them in the house, they shouldn't be visiting Hillel Gardens, to begin with."

It was weird, in Jamaica we were free to "gather" wherever we wanted, but here, organized parties were approved by the neighbourhood watch committee and couldn't be hosted after 10 pm because chilling on your lawn was considered "loitering".

Francis and his mother lived in a house historically owned by one of the "founding families" of the city. Originally built for a rich Toronto socialite, Francis' maternal great-grandfather purchased it years later and left it behind for Mrs. Porter after he passed away. We walked into the obnoxiously huge dwelling place where we were greeted by the smell of freshly baked chocolate chip cookies and his overly cheery mother.

"Hellooo kids! How was school?" Mrs. Porter asked as she placed the freshest batch of cookies on the counter.

"It was great, Mom, thanks for asking. How were the young adult intellectuals today?" Francis replied, reaching out for two cookies.

"As intellectual as ever . . ." she giggled and poured herself a giant glass of wine.

She was a university professor who didn't really have to work, but after divorcing Francis' dad, she went back to work "for fun". It always perplexed me how unusually polite Francis and his mother were to each other.

Maybe this is what the ideal mother-child relationship looks like, I thought to myself.

It could've also been a coping mechanism for what they've gone through. I mean seriously, how close could they really be when she didn't even know her son wasn't supposed to be at school today? Francis spoke little about his parents, but he told me they got divorced when he was eight. I sensed his discomfort in even telling me that much, so I never asked him the reason for the divorce and he never offered the information.

"Hi Mrs. Porter," I greeted her, holding my breath.

"You know, Emily, one of my students told me about this novel." She squinted hard, but the Botox in her forehead stayed porcelain. "I don't know if you've heard of it: *Makes me Wanna Holler* by Nathan McCall."

Here she goes again.

This time I didn't even try to hide my eye-rolling. By day, Mrs. Jill Porter was a professor of philosophy at the University of Toronto, St. George campus, but her side hustle was being a "Black-ologist." The very first time I met her at a "family get together", Francis invited me to, she sang the Negro National Anthem "Lift Every Voice and Sing" during a game of Song/Word Association . . . She got the word "lift".

On the surface, she was a very classy, poised and proper lady, but she had an odd obsession with topics relating to African-American and Black culture that made me feel uneasy.

"Yes, I have read it actually," I said, stifling a kiss teeth.

"I bought it on Kindle just a few hours ago," she said. "I can't wait to read it. My students warned me though, there's some foul language in it, like the use of the N-word." She gave me a wink.

I laughed sheepishly. "Well, let me know what you think, Mrs. Porter."

Francis, sensing my usual discomfort, ended the conversation before it got more awkward. "Okay mom, Emily and I . . . are going up . . . to my room." He said it like a robot every time.

She nodded and winked at me before waving us off. A perplexed expression unfolded across my face and before I could shoot Francis a stern look, he grabbed two more cookies and my hand, leading us to the staircase. When we were almost completely up the stairs, Mrs. Porter started playing her favourite playlist, *Impress the Black Kid.* Track one: *"F*ck the Police"* by NWA.

I peered at her through the pearl white bannister rails and shook my head at her nerdy dancing. Her long, blonde ponytail swished from side to side. *Like mother, like son, I guess.*

Francis rolled his eyes as we entered his room and closed the door behind him.

"Why does your mom always do that?" I asked. I usually ignore it and just write away my frustrations in my journal, but today I felt like being vocal, especially after having to read old boy Francis to filth earlier.

He shook his head, "I just don't understand how it's taken you this long to comment on it, you being you," he said.

I ignored his smart-ass remark. "Because I'm polite," I said matter-of-factly with a shrug.

"I don't know why she's like this," he said, responding to my question. He kicked over a piece of looseleaf paper, laying on the floor near his desk. He snorted, looked up at me and said, "But isn't it interesting that my mother is blacker than yours?"

My eyes narrowed as I stared at Francis's pale, white cheeks turn instantly fiery red. Showing that he put his foot in his mouth . . . again. He played with his dirty blond hair nervously.

"You know what I mean," he said.

I sighed, "No Francis, I don't know what you mean. I never know what you mean."

My comment prompted a minute of awkward silence. "So let me hear the newest poem."

"Why do you think there's a poem?"

I gave him a knowing look.

"Ok man, here it is." He handed me his classic black Moleskine and pointed to the right page. I took the red ribbon bookmark out and started reading it aloud.

Mistakes I've made.

Misunderstood I've been.

Experiences I've encountered in this life of sin.

I want to undo all the wrongs I've done

All the losses I should have won

Universe, if you're hearing me

Grant me a do-over, please

This life of guilt I'm living

Is making me weak to my knees.

I closed the book. "Do you know what it is about?" I asked.

"I'm not sure," he said.

"Hmm," I responded.

He was staring off into space. "I honestly don't know. I just feel lost lately." He offered.

I was quiet for a while. "Maybe this is about your dad, but why would you feel guilty?" I was grasping at straws. "The divorce was definitely not your fault. Do you feel like it was?"

He sighed and plopped himself down on his king-size bed. He grabbed his pillow with the green Egyptian cotton pillowcase. "I don't know, Em, maybe," he said.

I sat where his feet hung over the bed and reached back for his fingers. Sometimes when we were both feeling really down, I'd hold on to his hand. Just for a moment, he'd hold on to mine.

"Yea, maybe it's about him, I don't know," he said after a few seconds of thinking.

He sat up and met my gaze when I looked at him over my shoulder. He placed his left palm on my right hand. My heart pounded, and he stared into my eyes. He had this weird way of entering my soul with just one look. His long, soft fingers played with the tight tendrils of my hair as he tucked it behind my ear.

Then he opened his mouth to say something . . .

"Emily, your mom is here!" Mrs. Porter yelled from downstairs.

Her holler broke our gaze away from each other and we both laughed.

***

I hopped into the silver Mercedes Benz Compact SUV and closed the door. Reaching for my seatbelt, I barely had it on before my mother sped off like a criminal driving a getaway car at a robbery.

I took a deep breath in; being alone with my mom in an isolating car was unbearable when she was in a foul mood. "Good Afternoon, mommy",

I said, finally buckling my seat belt and ignoring her usual passive-aggressive demeanour.

Her brows furrowed, as if she smelled something horrible. Avoiding eye contact with me, confirming my assumption.

No response.

Yep, typical. She didn't even bother to ask me how my day was. I thought to myself, blankly staring in her direction. Well, two could play this game. In fact, I was better at it than she was. I put my Skullcandy headphones on and resumed the playlist I was listening to before I met up with Francis. I restarted Freddie McGregor's *"Push Come to Shove"*. My head started nodding along to the smooth riddim.

"What have I told you about having those headphones on when you're in the car, Emily?"

I jumped up at the sound of her scolding over the music.

"It is incredibly impolite." She quickly glanced at me and then returned to keep her eyes on the road.

I paused the track, turned my beaten-up rose gold Bluetooth headphones off and placed them in my backpack. Now there was silence, and the sound of the tires rumbling over the concrete was deafening.

"I told you to come home right after the event at school," she said stoically.

I ignored her demand. "How did you know I was with Francis?"

"Aren't you always?"

When she gets like this, it's best to just keep quiet, I told myself. It's not like she wants to hear what I have to say.

She locked her eyes on a stop sign at the beginning of our street.

Yep, that's right, mom. Francis and I are madly in lust, and each day I go to his house to engage in actions way beyond my years. I thought, knowing better than to say the actual words out loud. "He is just my friend, mother," I said instead.

How is she going to be mad at me for having a friend when she is the one who moved me away from all my friends? I vented in my mind.

"A young lady needs female friends and all I know is, girls who only hang out with boys have terrible reputations. You mus' know how you want to be perceived, Emily."

I rolled my eyes and stared out the window.

"If you would just lay your edges and maybe straighten your hair once in a while, you could highlight your beauty and maybe find some friends . . . like Katherine!"

When she said her name, tiny fireballs shot through my veins.

"She's such a sweet girl. Why don't you hang out with her more often?"

I shifted my gaze from the window and rotated my head slowly to face her. "Are you serious, mommy?" I shook my head and chuckled to myself.

My mom fell in love with Katherine the day Trinity assigned her as my "welcome buddy". For the first month of school, Katherine ushered me around, showed me where my classes were and let me sit at her table for lunch. I thought I made a group of new Canadian friends, but I found out Katherine had different plans.

"Since you and I are hanging out now, my mother wants to meet your parents to make sure . . . your family is . . . you know." Katherine said, through bites of cafeteria pizza.

It was my fifth time eating lunch with the clique of girls. "Cool, I'll talk to my parents . . . should we bring anything?" I asked, taking a gulp of apple juice. I looked around the table at each girl giggling to themselves.

"Why would you bring dinner . . . if I'm inviting you over for dinner, Emily." She scoffed at my offer. "We have caterers for that . . . what would you bring over, anyway."

Now the giggles turned into laughter.

"Well, my dad makes a great curried chicken." I replied.

"Ew, no. Just have your mom call mine and we will give you the details." Katherine waved off my suggestion and dove back into the pizza slice.

After lunch that day, I overheard Katherine tell the group that being nice to me was part of her community service hours for the year . . . I told my mother and I haven't trusted Katherine since.

Regardless of what Katherine said, my mother was still ecstatic to eat at the Caldwell's house. While Katherine and I decided being friends was overrated, our mothers became acquaintances. Because of that "charity dinner", Katherine's mom offered mine a job and soon after that we moved into the neighbourhood. Katherine hasn't let me forget it since.

To say that my mother and I have a complicated relationship would put it mildly. In fact, I couldn't recall a recent memory of a cordial conversation. I had spent my entire life deciphering why she was the way she was. When I journal about it, I compare our relationship to the toxic relationship she has with my grandma.

Weeks before we left Jamaica, I woke up to loud yelling.

"I am so sick of you telling me how to raise my child! Where was all of this energy when you were raising me?" I heard my mom scream.

"Not again . . ." I moaned, annoyed that my mom totally stole my "Where was all this energy line" that I used in an argument with her.

"I brought you up the best way I knew how, Marjorie. How dare you speak to me with such hate," my grandma said as calmly as she could, but I could still hear the hurt from upstairs.

"Yes, of course. Marjorie is always the terrible person, the ungrateful person. Mama, you can never acknowledge your flaws. I am so sick of this shit."

"Marjorie, please don't speak to your mother like that," I heard my dad chime in.

"Shut up, Frank! You're the next one! It is so funny to me that the two key people in my life never support me. Neither of you tries to understand where my hurt is coming from."

There was silence for about a minute.

"I didn't come here for this. I'm going to wake Emily and get going," my grandma said. I heard my grandma take a few steps.

Lowering her voice to a whisper, my mother replied, "You are not taking my child anywhere just so you can continue to fill her head with negative thoughts about me! You are the reason she and I don't have a good relationship. You are filling her head with so many lies! What kind of mother, what kind of person are you?"

There were about thirty seconds of silence.

"The only sad part about you moving to Canada is that you will take my grandchild. You are the toxic person, Marjorie . . . toxic! You are exactly like your father."

"I revel in the compliment, mother. My father was a wonderful person. You wish you could be half as good a person as he was."

I thought about getting up and going downstairs, but I felt paralyzed. Tears crawled to the surface of my eyelids as I sat up. Using the end of my white oversized t-shirt, I wiped the tears away, wishing they would stop.

My entire childhood was like a big nimbostratus cloud pouring buckets of toxic rain onto my head. When is it going to stop pouring? At least moving to Canada meant not having to deal with their fighting.

"Marjorie," my grandmother continued. "I hate to speak ill of the dead, but you, like your father, are a coward. You are so wrapped up in what everyone thinks of you instead of taking the time to find yourself, to love yourself truly. Have you ever, just for one moment, stopped to think about why you care so much about what other people think about you? Have you ever wondered why you are so desperate to fit in, so obsessed with belonging instead of standing out? You will fit right in, in Canada. It will be much easier for you to conform and hide from who you really are."

"Stop psychoanalyzing me, Mama! I hate when you do that!" I winced at the sound of my mother's voice cracking. She was clearly holding back tears, and it broke my heart. Were they really going to depart from each other without fixing things between them?

"You know exactly what I am talking about. You named your daughter Emily. Emily! A white-washed name. Why? Because you want her to fit in and not stand out. You want her to be lost in a sea of capitalistic robots instead of finding her true path."

"What is wrong with fitting in?" My mother asked. "What is wrong with wanting to belong?"

"Guys, enough, please," my dad tried to calm the arguing.

I heard one of the walnut-coloured counter stools screech against the tiled floor as someone got up.

"I'm getting Emily," she said. I heard footsteps coming up the stairs. Instinctively, I flung my head back on the black satin pillowcase and pretended to sleep, my back turned to my bedroom door.

"Em, sweetie, it's grandma . . . wake up." She whispered and stroked my cheek. "I'm here to pick you up for the book club. We're reading the autobiography of Malcolm X, tonight."

With an Oscar-nominated performance, I opened my eyes slowly and rubbed them. "Hi Grandma," I said in my best sleepy voice. "I'll go get ready."

"I'll be in the car," she said as she headed out the bedroom door swiftly. I'm not sure if it was the sleep hindering my sight, but I believe I saw a faint tear running down her left cheek.

It was moments like this, sitting with my mom in the car, that I wondered if we would end up like them.

"Seriously, Mommy, I don't understand your constant need to push me into having female friends, especially after your experiences with them."

"Oh, so you think Francis will not betray or hurt you?" She said matter-of-factly as she dramatically made a final left turn using the hand-over-hand method. "Emily, life is full of disappointments," she said as she came to a sudden halt at a stop sign and flicked on her right indicator. She muttered under her breath and kissed her teeth impatiently as two Trinity students crossed the street, forcing her to wait. After they crossed, she said, "What was I saying again? Oh yes! Male or female friends will come and go, but you cannot surround yourself with males only. You are a young woman. You're going through changes. Sure, I have had unpleasant experiences with some friends, but I learned a lot about myself." She beat on her chest aggressively. "Every experience is an opportunity to learn something. You need people by your side who you can talk to and learn from."

I am going through changes? I'm sixteen, almost seventeen, and now is the time she discusses puberty. "Isn't that what I have you for?" I asked sarcastically, peering at her from the corner of my eyes.

I saw her big dark brown eyes roll behind her brown Tom Ford oversized cat eyeglasses. "You're as stubborn as your father," she remarked as she drove into the driveway of an obnoxiously enormous house that we had the pleasure of calling ours for the last two years. She opened the deep mahogany double garage door and neatly slid her vehicle into the house.

Pushing my hand against the cream leather interior, I unlocked the door and exited the car.

"What do you want for dinner?" mom asked, closing the front door behind me.

"It's Friday remember, it's movie night with dad," I replied as I turned to face her.

"Oh, right . . . okay, you two kids can fend for yourself then," she said, rolling her eyes and heading to the kitchen.

I cannot deal with her attitude right now. "Okay, mom, whatever you say," I said and continued on the path to my room. I flung my backpack on the white faux fur rug by my bed and collapsed. I loved my room. It was the only place I felt so at peace. I took a deep breath in and let out all the frustrations from the day. But flashes of the woman from the fire popped up in my mind. "I didn't even ask her name," I mumbled to myself as I smacked my face with my hand. Something about that woman made my heart so heavy. After a few minutes, I got up and headed to my desk.

I needed to write this all out. I took my journal out of my backpack, turned my desk light on, and began writing.

SEPTEMBER 17, 2016 8:35 PM,

Weird things happened today . . . And it's making my mind reel in circles. Is Canada really somewhere I can truly be happy? Is Trinity the best place for me? Is Francis a good friend?

If Francis really was a good friend, why didn't he care when I told him about the woman and the fire? Was he really that insensitive?

Also Girl's Day was so pointless, man. I should have followed my gut and stayed home. The biggest problem with Girls' Day was that there was no representation of any other race. That is not real feminism, and to be honest, a part of me thinks they set it up that way on purpose. Before the assembly we had a "breakfast party" . . . such a weird concept.

Katherine and her little friend Olivia came to sit with me. Katherine asked me, "Why are you eating alone, loner?" to which I replied, "Who else am I supposed to eat with?" My initial reaction was to pay her no mind and continue eating my berries and kiwi, but they literally stayed hawking over me like crows.

So eventually I asked them: "Girls, is there something I can help you with?"

Taking that as an invitation to sit down, Katherine and her minion took a seat and said, "I think you have me all wrong, Emily. You fascinate me. I have met no one who is as passionate about something as you are." Katherine said with a grin.

I stared at her and picked up a blackberry with my plastic fork. Where was she going with this?

"What I don't like though is that you're not really fair." I guess she realized I had no intention of asking her what she meant because she continued. "You speak up for Black people, which is cool and everything, but what about all the other races? Asians went through their own hardships. Whites did too, I mean, look at the Holocaust, and let's not even get into the treatment of Indigenous peoples. If your focus is really on promoting equality, then you should really protest that all lives matter."

Her little sidekick nodded in agreement.

I sighed. Here we go again. I looked up at her and with the fakest smile I could muscle up, I said, "Katherine, I appreciate your honesty and I admire how insightful you are, but let us get one thing straight. All lives don't matter if black lives don't matter." I finished the bite left on my fork and then asked her, "Are you going to move or should I?"

She stared at me like I stole her man, while Olivia stared at her with bated breath, waiting for her response. "Of course I think black lives matter. After all, my mom got your mom a better-paying job when you guys were fresh off the boat . . . that's the only reason you live where you live."

There were so many reasons to loathe Katherine, but the biggest reason was how she made me feel. Yes, her mom got my mom a better job, but I'm not a damn charity case! I darted a seriously cold look her way, warning her to move. She didn't make any movement, so I packed up my half eaten fruits, walked away and left her with her thoughts.

This girl mus' ti'yad fi'mi walk weh from her. I can't stand her!

Just then, my phone went off in my pocket. Twitter interrupted my journaling. *Ding, Ding, Ding!*

I let out a laugh as my childhood friend George defended me from a Twitter troll.

Ding! The notification read: **FKPorter** just tweeted.

When I clicked on his tweet, it was easy to see that Francis "King" Porter was flying high from his journalistic endeavours earlier. At his peak hour on Twitter, he posted a few more shots from the fire. A photo of Francis standing beside the city's Chief of Police popped up with a few photos of students from our school. With the apartment building burning down behind them, Francis took a group selfie with Katherine and a few others from Trinity. The caption read . . .

I slammed my phone down. I didn't even know Katherine was there and why were they taking a selfie with the Chief of Police while families were evacuating their homes?

Overwhelmed by the bullshit, I shut my journal with force.

Ding!

"Mi done wid social media for today!" I exclaimed before noticing it was my dad texting me.

Running late. Order whatever you want, I'm down for anything.

I laughed. *My dad swears he's the coolest person alive.* I pulled up my

Uber Eats app and started scrolling through options until I finally decided on a restaurant. "Pizza it is!"

CHAPTER 4

MOVIE NIGHT

I sat in the basement, excited as a child on Christmas Eve. Friday nights meant movie nights with dad. It was our time to recap the events of our week and just hang out like two teenagers. I anxiously awaited his return home from work, setting out snacks we both loved. Sweet and salty popcorn, Cheetos Puffs, white chocolate macadamia nut cookies, double stuffed Oreos and, of course, a large Meat Lover's pizza from our favourite pizza parlour.

When I heard his keys jingle as he entered the house, I sprung from the table and ran towards the foot of the carpeted staircase leading to our foyer.

"I smell Little Ceasars!" He shouted from the top of the stairs. Dad galloped down, and I rushed over to plug the HDMI cord into the TV. Eyeing the table of junk food, he scoffed jokingly as he placed his work bag on the floor near the stocked mini-fridge. "What happened to the vegan challenge we're supposed to do, Em?" He asked with a laugh, eyeing the spread but focusing on the pizza.

My daddy had the most infectious laughter, which I inherited, along with his malocclusion. *Thank goodness for braces!*

"That vegan challenge was *grandma's* suggestion. I didn't agree with it," I laughed and shrugged my shoulders.

Just then, my mom came trudging down the stairs. "I came down to see if you guys wanted me to whip something up for dinner," she said again but directed it to daddy this time. Clearly an excuse to intrude on the weekly father-daughter movie night. She stood at the bottom of the stairs, close to the mini-fridge where my dad was now, crouched down, getting a Heineken.

At first glance, they looked like the picture-perfect couple. Physically, they were both very attractive. My mother's dark, rich complexion complimented her dark brown eyes. She showed her dedication to the gym through her slender yet fit physique. Standing at 5 feet 6 inches, she had thick, bouncy, shoulder-length coils which we rarely saw because she always wore her hair bone straight, ever since Mrs. Caldwell suggested it.

Why not just get a relaxer?

My dad was 6'2 but had the same silky skin tone as my mother. But the appearance of perfection was where the "relationship goals" ended. Though they never said it, I was pretty sure my parents stayed together just for my sake, or to avoid the inconvenience that came along with divorce. They constantly spoke to each other in callous tones, with no sign of love or adoration for each other.

"No thanks, Mom," I said, pointing to the pizza.

"Okay, well, I can make some cookies or something," she replied.

"Marjorie, we're fine. Thank you," my dad said stiffly.

I always felt a minute twinge of guilt when my dad spoke so coldly to my mom. We may not get along, but she's my mom, after all.

Tail between her legs, she said, "Okay, fine Frank, I was just offering…" and stormed up the stairs.

Dad ignored her. "How was school today, princess?"

The basement door slammed behind my mother and I shuddered before answering. "It was good, it was kinda weird…" my voice trailed off because I hadn't admitted it out loud until just now.

"What was so weird about it?" He said, reaching for a handful of Cheetos, eyes glued to the TV.

"Did you hear about the fire on Bloor?" I said.

"Yes…" he said hesitantly, as if he was expecting trouble. "Please don't tell me you went down there to see it. I saw it on the news at work and it was chaos down there." He reproached.

"I did, but I didn't go close or anything. Francis was there to cover it for his newspaper submission, so I followed him."

My dad's arms folded across his chest as he urged me to continue.

"Well, there was this lady who needed help . . . it looked like she lost her home in the fire." I looked down at the half-eaten macadamia nut cookie laying on the napkin in front of me.

"And . . ." his voice got a little more stern.

"So I used my emergency card to book a room for her, at the holiday inn." I blurted. "She had two kids with her, dad."

My dad looked at me with his kind eyes and then pulled me into his chest. "Em, next time you call me to help. That card is for your emergencies."

"Dad, I had to help her." I looked up at his chin.

"That's okay, but how can we truly help this woman, without you using your credit card?" He asked, but no ideas came to my mind. "Write about it, bring light to the situation, call your classmates to action. Maybe this is something your school could help with . . . like a community project." My dad always had the best solutions.

"That's funny you say that because I was thinking about trying out for the newspaper this year," I said hesitantly.

"That's great! You should. You already know I think you're an amazing writer."

"I doubt if I'll make the team, though, and I don't even know if I really want to. What if I'm stuck writing fluffy pieces I don't care about?" I said, biting into the soft-baked cookie.

"Well, I think you should try out and when you make the team, implement some changes. You are just as important in that school as they are. Let them hear your voice. Momento Audere Semper!" My dad was an alumnus of my old high school, and a proud one at that.

"Yes, Momento Audere Semper! You're right. I will work on my submission piece tomorrow. So how was work?" I asked, really, to change the subject. My dad was a Senior Accounting Manager at Canada's Commerce Bank.

"It was okay," he replied.

"Just okay?" I inquired.

"Just okay. Absolutely nothing special," He said after taking a sip of his beer. "One interesting thing happened though, I think my manager is prejudiced," he said casually.

"Oh, really? Tell me more," I said, my ears perking up. I grabbed some Cheetos Puffs from the family-sized bag so I could really focus on the story.

He laughed, "Well, you've heard me talk about my work, bredrin, Phillip. I don't know if I ever mentioned that he's Filipino. Well, Phillip has been working for the bank for ten years. He told me today that Mr. Allen said to him that now is not the right time for him to get a promotion."

"That's it?" I asked, visibly confused. "Why do you guys think that's prejudice?" My face scrunched up as I asked the question.

Dad looked up at me, "Because the next day, Sean, a new guy and nephew of the boss, received the promotion instead."

Wow, daddy sure knows how to bury the lead. I thought to myself.

"So what's Phillip going to do?"

"Nothing," my dad said as he took a slice of pizza.

"Nothing? He is just going to continue working there?"

"Well, he's actively applying for jobs in the position he wants."

Seeing my facial expression, my dad spoke up, "Just let it go, Emily. This is not your fight."

"Fine," I huffed. I filled my mouth with the remaining five Cheetos in my hand.

"So what are we watching tonight?" Dad said.

"Two choices, we have 'Set it Off' and 'American Gangster'."

"Oh, that's the mood we are in?" he laughed. "Okay, let's go with American Gangster."

My dad was the biggest Denzel fan, so it did not surprise me he chose that movie.

"Okay, let's go." I pressed play and grabbed three slices of pizza, one for myself and two for dad.

Frank Morrison, my father, fondly known by his peers as Frankie, was my best friend. We always had a close relationship and started our movie nights when we first moved to Canada. He was having difficulty finding a job and he started assisting me with my assignments. In the end, we would curl up on the sofa and talk about everything from his childhood to how many kids he originally wanted. There is no story more entertaining than a Jamaican's childhood.

We watched the movie and ate profusely; it was complete bliss. My favourite scene from the movie appeared brightly on the TV screen. Frank Lucas (Denzel Washington) walked out of the church and realized the police cornered him.

I grabbed my phone and opened Twitter.

Emily Morrison
@EmWrites

...

Only Denzel Washington can play a role as a villain and have you hoping the villain wins in the end. And yes, I know American Gangster is based on a true story so don't @ me.

8:00 · 2016 · Twitter Web App

14 Retweets   **10** Quote Tweets   **15** Likes

I pressed the bright blue "Tweet button" and sent my witty thoughts into the Twitter atmosphere.

Ding! Ding! Ding! A few seconds later, after placing my phone on the couch, I saw two notifications from Twitter.

TDOTGIRL retweeted.

That social handle popped up a lot lately. When the movie ended, I looked at my dad. "Can I ask you a question?"

"Sure, Boops," he replied in a cheery tone. "Boops" was the nickname he gave me when I wasn't even old enough to say it.

"Do you love mom?"

He turned uncomfortably on the sofa and faced me. He and the rest of my family called it a "seettee". "Why do you ask?" He inquired.

"If you did, you would have said yes," I said, looking him dead in the eyes. He laughed, "You really think you're so wise, don't you?"

I stared at him, waiting for the answer. "Yes, I love your mother," he said. "Why do you ask?"

"Because you guys don't talk to each other like you're in love," I responded.

"Emily," he said, shifting on the seettee, "You will learn as you get older that there is a difference between loving someone and being in love with someone. I love your mother very much, but are we in love? That is a question to be answered another day."

"Why do questions always have to be answered another day?" I asked at the risk of sounding like a teen television sitcom, "I am sixteen years old and I really think I am old enough to have this conversation."

"Well, mi nuh ready," he replied bluntly. "Just give me some time and I will come back to you, *zeen*?"

I kissed my teeth. "Fine," I said reluctantly. "I'm tired. I can't walk up the stairs," I whined after a few minutes.

He laughed, "You're so damn lazy." He picked me up and flung me over his shoulder.

"Works every damn time. Don't stop lifting those weights, Dad," I chuckled, kissing him on the cheek.

CHAPTER 5
SUBMISSION PIECE #2

The sun peered through the venetian blinds, hugging the bay windows in my bedroom. Being a natural morning person, I jumped out of bed feeling enthusiastic. Picking up my phone, resting on the nightstand near my bed, I pulled up my morning playlist. Tunes pumped out of the speaker and soon every soca song I loved throughout the years guided my hips, swinging from side to side. Making my way towards the bathroom, I eased down onto the ice cold toilet seat and scrolled through Instagram while my playlist blasted through the magenta wireless speakers. Then, I turned on the shower and let the water get to the right temperature. Hot! What was supposed to be a quick shower with my favourite body wash, Nubian chai and goat's milk, became a 45 minute carnival fete. I was giving cheers to life, as Voice instructed. I came out to a party, just like Shal Marshall, and I gyrated like I was high off the booze to "Bambilambambilambilambam" by Farmer Nappy. It was a total weekend vibe with complete bliss; just what I needed to get the day started.

I got out of the shower, soaked from coils to toe. I dried my body with my grey oversized towel, took my satin black robe off the hanger behind my bathroom door and covered my nakedness. With soca still bumping in the background, I applied Jamaican Black Castor Oil Leave-in Conditioner onto my damp tresses from roots to ends and sealed in the moisture with my homemade whipped shea butter and grapeseed oil. After moisturizing and sealing each section, I put them in jumbo twists. I then slathered some whipped butter on my entire body, grabbed black cotton underwear from my drawer and then some "yard clothes", which is really just "going out clothes" that Jamaicans no longer considered good enough to be worn out. As I quickly covered my glistening melanated body with denim shorts and light pink crew neck sweater, I thought about what I would eat for breakfast.

Hastily, I made my way down the dark varnished-wooden staircase and into the kitchen. By this point I unplugged my headphones and switched to listening to the music out loud.

My mother's kitchen resembled a photograph from an interior design magazine. Surrounded by dark brown modern cupboards and drawers, sat an onyx coloured island with a white marble countertop. I opened one pantry and removed the plastic cereal storage containing *Honey Nut Cheerios*. Then I took an emerald coloured cereal bowl from a cupboard on the right side of the kitchen, a metal spoon from a drawer directly beneath the cupboard and the almond milk from the refrigerator. Combining the two ingredients, I began munching away. The spoon screeched loudly as it grazed the bowl until there was nothing left but cheerios dregs. I nodded to the beat of the playing song *"People,"* by Kes, as I washed the kitchenware and placed them on the drainer to dry. I was ready to relax in the living room when . . . *Ding! Ding! Ding!*

Francis sent me a photo on iMessage. I waited for the image to load before gasping out loud when it finally did. Covering my mouth, I studied the photo, my eyes darted from left-to-right, reading the headline in bold black letters:

"JAMAICAN WOMAN FIGHTING DEPORTATION AFTER OVERSTAYING HER VISITOR VISA."

In the centre of the photo, was the familiar terrified expression of the woman who followed me to the hotel after the fire. Her eyes were staring straight into the lens of the camera as she clutched onto the little hands of her children. A gigantic man in a police uniform had his hand on her shoulder as they moved towards an industrial looking building.

Ding! A message from Francis followed.

Hey, is she the lady you brought to the hotel?

It surprised me. I guess Francis was actually listening to me when I described her. I bolted back to my bedroom and shut the door behind me. Frantically, I googled the number for the hotel and called to the front desk of the Holiday Inn.

Ring, Ring, Ring! My heart felt as if it would jump out of my chest.

"Hello, Holiday Inn, Jan speaking. How can I help you?" A jolly voice sing-songed into the phone.

"Uh, hi, yes . . . I checked in with my . . . aunt yesterday . . . room 407. I just wanted to know if she checked out or–"

"Oh yes! I remember you!" The voice interrupted. "Miss Morrison?"

"Yes, yes, that's me." I said urgently.

"Oh yes, Miss Morrison, your aunt has checked out already." The voice replied.

"Okay, thanks . . . " I said, my voice trailing off into silence.

"Is there anything else I can do for you, Miss Morrison?" the voice offered.

"Uh, nope . . . no, thank you." I ended the call. Blankly staring at my laptop, I sat in my desk chair, stunned. My body felt like springing into action, while my mind kept replaying Francis' words, *You can't take on someone else's stuff, Emily.*

I tried to process what had just happened. That lady was in more trouble than I thought. Something in me had to find her, but I kept thinking there was nothing I could do to help. I looked back down at the image. The woman's eyes looked exhausted. There was a deeper story to that apartment fire, a story that I could probably help to uncover.

Emily, are you serious? I imagined Francis already scoffing at my attempt to do something altruistic. *What can one teenage girl do?* Lately, every ounce of self-doubt playing in my head had Francis's voice attached to it. As I cleared off my desk overflowing with loose leaf paper, I had a thought. Maybe I was just one teenage girl, but what if my dad was right? What if I could help this lady by writing about what was happening to her? I geared my brain towards writing my paper when I realized I had no clue where to begin. My writer's block was in full force and suddenly my day transitioned from perfect to frustrating. I turned away from my laptop and reached for my journal.

I'll just start at the beginning . . . I placed my pen gently in between two pages, as a bookmark, and let my thoughts go on their own path.

"Remember the last time you felt brave?" I whispered my DIY writing prompt to myself. I closed my eyes, transporting myself back home. Where the sun kissed my skin and the tropical breeze blew in from the wooden doors at the entrance of my old church.

At the Golden Seas United Brethren Church, I stood beside the white-varnished pulpit beaming with pride and feeling honoured at the same time. Signalling the musicians, I was about to sing! They started with a jazzy instrumental intro of *"God Rest Ye,"* and when my cue hit, I slowly, smoothly let out the chorus. All eyes were on me, as each member of the congregation sat, captivated by every run, melody and lyric that came out of my mouth. Although I was only six years old, I knew God blessed me with a gift to minister to people through song. It was Christmas Sunday and the clergy heavily decorated the very humble bungalow style church with Christmas ornaments. They displayed a large Christmas tree in the centre of the church with a cross at its peak, and behind it was a festively decorated offering table. Colourful wreaths hung on the entrance doors, and "pepper lights" hung from the wooden pulpit railings. I was the final "Ministry" on the program, before the sermon. At six I had so much confidence, I was just being the star that I was.

Standing with the microphone safely in my hands, I sang a medley of Christmas carols I arranged. It was composed of *"The Little Drummer Boy"*, *"God Rest Ye"*, and of course *"Oh Holy Night."* I rehearsed with the band for three weeks and I was ready for my 2nd annual Christmas debut. There I stood with no nerves in my red and white tulle Christmas dress, white stockings and white low chunky heels. My mother neatly combed my hair in a half up, half down hairstyle that was achieved from large cornrows that were braided the day before. My three-minute performance finished with a powerful vibrato and at the end, the congregation greeted me with a roaring sea of applause and a standing ovation. I beamed with happiness and pride. When my father escorted me off the stage, I sat in the front row beside him. We sat there for the rest of the service, and I sat in awe at the reaction I received. I felt so proud of myself, and it filled me with immense gratitude. I was pretty much mentally writing my Grammy acceptance speech for best Gospel Singer in my head. At the end of the service, a lot of church members complimented me on my humility and bravery on stage. Most of the comments expressed their awe that a little girl like me wasn't scared to go up on the pulpit, sing by myself and to top it all off, sing so professionally. There was one person, however, Sister Rowe, whose compliment I will always remember.

"You did exceptionally well, Emily, as usual," she said. "But there is something I want you to never forget. Not everyone will hear your voice and understand the potential you have or the impact you can make, but you need to always remember how gifted you are. Allow no one to dim your light, especially so theirs can shine brighter."

I think about this memory often. I didn't understand it at first, but I certainly did now ...

***

I opened my eyes and turned on my laptop for a second time. I pulled up a blank document and typed out the title of my article, "HOMES GO UP IN FLAMES . . . LET'S TAKE A SELFIE."

Yes, yes, that's it!

The words spewed out of my fingertips without hesitation and in an hour the piece basically wrote itself. I saved it on my desktop as "Oracle Submission Piece" and printed out a copy for my dad to proofread later. Crashing on my bed, I looked at the left over bag of Cheetos puffs from last night and curled up in the blankets.

Was the woman somewhere warm? I tried to suppress the thought.

I picked up the TV remote from the nightstand to the right of my bed, turned the TV on and clicked on *"Sister Sister"*.

Were her children safe? I tried to clear my head and forget about it again.

As I lay on my very comfortable bed re-watching an episode I had watched many times, I felt completely at peace . . . for a second.

I wonder where she is? Why was I so bothered by this?

A funny and familiar clip made me laugh hysterically, even though I knew it was coming. But there wasn't any use . . . not even Tia, Tamera, Lisa, and Jordan could make me forget about this. But what could I do right now about it? I thought to myself. I continued watching the series until the series ended up watching me.

The next day, I woke up in a great mood. I had written a piece that I was proud of, but I wondered if the Oracle editor would find it fascinating. I was essentially putting classmates on blast and calling them to action, but the article was more than that. It highlighted my generation's need for external validation. It talked about entitlement and privilege; it touched on the families affected by the fire and my thoughts on how we could help. I was actually very excited to go to school tomorrow. As I did with every piece I've ever written, I showed my dad for constructive feedback.

"Dad!" I yelled as I walked the 2,850 word paper over to him.

"I'm downstairs in the kitchen," he said.

"Good Morning, Daddy!" I said, kissing him on the cheek. "I wrote the piece!"

My dad was sitting on one of the bar stools having breakfast; fried dumplings, ackee saltfish, and Blue Mountain black coffee.

"Weh you nah seh! A dat you did inna you room a do the entire day, yesterday?" He teased through the dumpling bite.

The kitchen was his kingdom and with every meal, the room would heat up while reggae played in the background. My favourite sight to see was my dad moving to the music while cooking with the burner on high.

"Yep. Please read and critique as per usual," I said in my most professional voice as I handed him the paper.

"Good Morning, Emily," my mother said as she entered the kitchen wearing her long black robe that was the adult version of mine.

"Good Morning, Mom," I said.

"What's that?" she asked both of us as she poured herself a cup of coffee.

"It's Emily's submission piece for the school newspaper," my dad replied stiffly as he watched my shoulders tense up.

I spun the bar stool around, my back facing the parentals, and stared at the floor. I hoped my dad would finish reading quickly . . . *I could always get his feedback later today.*

"Oh, I want to read it when you're done, Frank," she said excitedly. Receiving no response, she sipped her coffee in a matter-of-fact manner and asked me, "Is that alright with you, Emily?"

Everyone in that room knew there was only one right answer, so reluctantly, I mumbled, "Yes, that's fine." My head still down to the floor, bar stool spinning again.

Dad finished reading and attempted to place the paper on the island, but my mother quickly grabbed it from him in mid-air. Dad and I made eye contact in a split second.

"Emily, this is a really excellent piece," my dad spoke up.

"Thanks dad," I replied. "Which part of it do you think can be improved?" I asked.

"Well, for one," my mom interjected, "You used your credit card to book a hotel room for a stranger!"

Here we go.

"Mommy, she had kids. What would you do?" I pulled up the photo of the woman on my phone and showed her the article, bringing it close to her face.

She swiped it out of my hands. "Oh, even better she's probably going to end up in an immigrant detention centre now." She shook her head before handing the phone back to me.

"I asked for a critique of my article, not a critique on my personal decisions." I said, grabbing the phone from her and placing it in my back pocket.

"Well, you need to tone the article down, it's too aggressive." She said over her shoulder, focusing on the dishes in the sink.

"What do you mean?" I asked quizzically.

"Do you have a pen?"

I gave her the pen I brought down with the paper.

She circled the two last sentences in the first paragraph. "Take this out or rephrase it. This is way too controversial. You don't want to come across as the angry black girl, do you?" she asked rhetorically.

I leaned over the island and read the lines: *It's very important that in today's society, we as millennials, take an active role in standing up for equality. That means going beyond sharing, commenting, and liking a post.* "I don't understand what's wrong with those two sentences, mom," I said shyly. "I don't sense any anger, and I wasn't angry when I wrote it."

"Emily, your head is so tough. You need to learn to listen," she said as she continued circling and jotting notes beside words and sentences. "That's your problem. You asked for feedback and when you get it you don't want to take it. You need to learn to take constructive criticism."

Before I responded, my dad spun the bar stool around with a limp piece of ackee on his fork and faced her aggressively. His eyes fixated on her, "She asked *me* for feedback, she neva ask you nuttn'". He pushed the fork in his mouth and while chewing he continued, "Why do you always have to be so nuff?"

"Okay, okay guys, please let's not do this," I said, but that was pointless. They began their usual verbal equivalent of fist fighting. I took my butchered submission piece and my pen and slowly went upstairs, tail between my legs. As I climbed each step, I looked through tears at the sea of red ink that flooded my paper. None of the criticisms were constructive . . . it was clear she wanted me to change the entire paper. Returning to my room, I felt exceptionally low. I sat around my desk, connected my headphones to my phone, and turned on my "90s-2000s R&B playlist" to drown out the venomous arguing that ensued downstairs because of my article. A few minutes ago I was on cloud nine, so incredibly proud of a piece I had written, and within a matter of seconds my mother made me feel discouraged and beaten down. That was a record for her. I crumpled the paper and placed it in my black metal trash bin. Powering on my laptop, I opened a new document and titled it "SUBMISSION PIECE: #2."

CHAPTER 6

DITCHED

"I'm sitting . . . all the way . . . at the back," I mouthed while typing a response to Francis.

The red and white Toronto transit bus turned off of Lily Valley Drive and onto Rose Avenue, Francis' street. My legs hopped up and down in my khaki uniform pants while I anxiously awaited his arrival.

When he got on the bus, I watched him fight against school bags to get to the back, almost tripping on a duffle bag while he was at it. Using his navy blue tie to wipe off beads of sweat on his forehead, he finally made it to the seat I saved for him.

"You okay there, Porter?" I teased.

"These people don't know how to take off their backpacks on the bus, eh?"

I looked back at the group of people he strong-armed past. A woman in scrubs held her work bag over her shoulder and her child's backpack on the other as she placed her son in the chair in front of her. Across from her, two men carried construction hats under their arms and juggled their lunch bags with a duffle bag full of gear.

I looked back at Francis.

He caught my stare and nervously ran his hand through his hair. Reaching into his pocket with the other, he pulled out a pack of gum and waved it in front of me. "Want some?" he motioned, his sweaty hands clutched the minty chewing sticks.

"No, I'm good." I replied.

Ding! We both looked at our phones, but it was Francis' iPhone that needed his attention.

He pulled it out, opened the message and then quickly closed the screen, noticing I was watching him. Still breathing heavily from struggling on the bus, he looked over at me. "I thought you would have had it out waiting for me." His cheeks were a little flushed.

I ignored his irritated tone. "Here it is," I said as I took the original submission piece out of my hot pink binder. I wanted to see if my mom's critique was right, so I asked Francis to give me feedback, too.

His eyes danced from left to right, up and down, for about ten minutes before turning to face me with a blank stare. "Wow, so that's how you feel?" he inquired softly. "Is this the only piece you wrote?"

"Um, yea," I lied hesitantly.

"Hmm," he remarked.

"What does 'hmm' mean?" I asked as I moved my binder from a hugging position to lie flat in my lap.

"Promise you won't get mad?" he asked nervously.

"Nope, I can't promise you that," I said, shrugging my shoulders.

"This is way too controversial," he said. "What's this? You're putting your classmates on blast . . . you just sound bitter in this article."

That was it! He didn't care about the story at all. Once again, Francis made everything about his reputation. I pulled the cord, signalling the bus driver to not bypass the next stop. I'm sure he already knew because the next stop was Trinity and practically 75% of the passengers were Trinity students.

As the bus slowed down, I turned to Francis. "Excuse me."

He abruptly moved his knees out of my way as I marched towards the exit. In my peripheral vision, I saw his obnoxious eye roll. The bus stopped, and I pushed aggressively on two yellow handles on the door. Storming out, with no desire to look behind me.

"Em, can you just wait?" he asked in an annoyed tone.

I twirled around to face him.

"Okay, sit here with me for a sec," he said, pointing to a marble bench at the entrance of the school. "Okay, Em, look at this sentence," he said as he read the first paragraph. He cleared his throat before reading:

"As I saw the selfie of my classmates standing in front of the burning building, I couldn't help but think, it's our job to change the problematic way the generation before us thinks and how my generation currently behaves . . ."

Francis read it, mocking my tone. Lifting his eyes from the paper, he locked eyes with me. "You can say what you want to say without offending an entire generation, Em."

I grabbed my paper, not too hard as I didn't want it to tear. "I'm sorry," I said, with probably way too much attitude. "Is an opinion piece not supposed to have my opinion?" I asked sarcastically.

Sighing, Francis said, "So clearly you want more people to hate you here. You've called out every straight-A student in our grade, by name, in this article. You know what? Submit it. I don't care. But don't come crying to me when the Oracle doesn't choose your name as one of the fresh additions to the team." He got up and walked away just as the bell started ringing.

I watched him walk until he was out of sight, then slowly I unzipped my binder and placed the paper neatly on top of my second submission option. Maybe this article would piss off a few kids at school, but this story was more than that. I just wanted it to be a call to action.

Ding! Ding! I grabbed my phone from the front pocket of my bag and glanced at the screen to see an article written by the Toronto Globe Newspaper: IMMIGRANT WOMAN BEGS FOR HELP AS OFFICIALS DETAIN HER IN AN IMMIGRATION DETENTION CENTRE.

"Holy shit!" I blurted out.

Two science teachers glared at my outburst but kept walking towards the entrance of the school. After Francis sent me the article about the woman from the fire, I started following the story on Twitter. Quickly, I retweeted the article and asked my followers if they knew about any support for the woman.

Slogging through the school entrance and dragging myself to homeroom, I couldn't get this woman out of my mind. *Why did I feel so responsible for her?* I pushed the woman's sad expression out of my head and took a deep breath. Right now, I needed to focus on what I could control, and what I could control was making it to class on time.

For the rest of the day, I avoided walking past the Oracle office. I was confused about which article to submit. Was it possible that my mother and Francis were right? Was I just too obstinate to see it? My gut was telling me that my first piece was impactful. It highlighted issues that were woven into the culture of our society, this city and even this school. But I didn't need more hate . . . Francis was right.

When 2:30pm rolled around, the school day had finally ended.

Ding! At around 2:38pm, Francis sent me a text.

Want to bus home together?

I twiddled my thumbs, trying to decide what to say to him. Should I piss him off the way he did me earlier this morning, or should I be the bigger person?

Yea, sure. Meet you at the bus stop.

I typed back. I decided against bringing up the fact that I was going to take the plunge and submit the article now. I ran down the stairs instead of using the elevator and made my way to the first floor, where the matrix was located. It felt as if I crawled through the long-abandoned hallway, partly hoping that I would never reach my locker, because that would just confirm the reality that I still had the dilemma of deciding which piece to submit.

Arriving at my locker, I did my usual experimenting with the lock until it finally opened by itself. "Mi hate dis cheap piece a lock, enuh," I mumbled.

I checked my phone, 2:45pm. I had seven minutes to submit my piece and three minutes to catch the 2:55pm bus with Francis. At 2:50pm, I arrived at the mahogany coloured office door of the newspaper room, my hot pink binder closely bound to my chest. I stared at the large bold Arial font sign that read, "PLACE SUBMISSIONS BELOW" with a black bold paper arrow pointing to a tray. On the grey metal tray lay a pile of submitted articles. I gripped my binder even closer to my chest and tapped my right foot as I weighed the pros and cons for both article submissions. I took a deep breath in and exhaled every anxious thought. Opening the binder, I took the first article out and held the paper between my lips, using my lifted right knee as a support for closing the binder.

I was in mid submission when Katherine approached me.

"Hey, Emily! How was your weekend, girl?" she beamed.

I slowly slipped the article back into my binder and turned around to face her. I will never understand why Canadians care so much about each other's weekends. I never know if it's because they are genuinely interested or if they just want to brag. In Katherine's case, I was pretty sure it was the latter.

In Jamaica, when we saw someone on a Monday, it was "good morning" and we kept it moving. "Hi," I mumbled. "My weekend was amazing!" I said, exaggerating.

Her eyes drifted from my mocking expression and glanced over to the stack of papers in front of me. "Are you submitting an article?" she asked.

No, I just enjoy standing in front of random rooms when I have a bus to catch, I thought. *What kind of stupid question was that?* "Nope," I lied. "I'm actually just looking for Francis. Have you seen him?"

"Nope," she said. I looked up in her direction. She flipped her hair on both sides of her head, revealing a large, continent-shaped purple hickey on the right side of her neck.

A wah do this nasty gyal. Who flaunts a hickey?

When she caught me staring at it, she repeated herself. "No, Emily, I haven't seen him." Her eyes grazed over the contents of my hands.

"Have you submitted a piece?" I asked her, clinging to my property.

"Not yet. A friend of mine who is actually on the newspaper team is editing my submission article and then I'm going to reprint it when she's done and submit it," she said. Again, she flipped her hair back to show off her sex scar.

"Isn't that cheating?" I asked with a raised eyebrow.

"I like to call it networking, you know, kinda like affirmative action," she said and gave me a wink.

I raised my eyebrows, "Katherine, do you even know what affirmative action is?" I asked.

"Emily! Gosh, it was just a joke, don't get all Rosa Parks on me now."

"Hmm," was the only thing that I could say. I bit my lip, holding in the words I really wanted to speak. Pretending to check my cell phone, I realized there was a text from Francis. "Crap. Francis is at the bus stop, waiting for me. I have to go. See you later," I said, walking away briskly. I ran through the matrix to catch up to him. When I arrived at the bus stop, he was standing with his arms crossed, a frustrated expression plastered on his face. Before I could even say hi, his first question was, "Did you submit it?"

"Shoot," I said. "I forgot . . . Katherine came up to me, I was trying to avoid her and then it totally slipped my mind."

He rolled his eyes. "Will you stop blaming her for everything? Well, go hand it in! Hurry!" He looked really annoyed at this point.

Flustered by his attitude, I shook my head. "Okay, okay, I'm going," I yelled as I ran back in the direction I came from. I flung open Trinity's entrance door and sprinted to the newspaper office. This time, I was alone and had time to really think. When I successfully dropped the second version of my article on the pile I hoped I made the right decision. I booked it to my locker to drop off the binder with the other submission inside. I was tired of holding it in my arms and didn't have room for it in my backpack. Hurriedly, I swung the lock in the hole and fidgeted with the dial, pushing the lock up as far as it would go.

That's good enough, I thought.

Checking my phone, I saw it was 3:00pm . . . we had just missed the bus. I Usain Bolted out of the matrix to meet Francis so we could wait for the next 30 minutes until another bus arrived. But when I got there, Francis was nowhere to be found.

"I guess he was in a rush," I mumbled to myself, letting out an exasperated exhale. Pulling out my phone, I sent him a text.

Did you leave?

The three dots popped up as I waited for his stupid excuse, but then they disappeared. *What the heck? Why would he leave when he asked me to bus home with him?*

I was livid. Francis hadn't ever left me at the bus stop like this, not without an actual reason. Was he really that mad at me for writing about his selfie in my article? Maybe he really felt like I was calling him out. Just then, another wave of pubescent pupils flowed through the school's main entrance. I stood a few feet away from the stop, which was far away from the other kids, and took my headphones out of my bag. While the Bluetooth connected, I pulled up my "*Roots Reggae*" playlist and started playing the track "*Double Trouble*" by Beres Hammond. I let the September sun shine on my face, and my mood dissipated. I was really catching a vibe from the song when I lifted my head to see an unfamiliar face waving frantically, trying to get my attention. I pulled my headphones down and around my neck.

"Hi, you're Emily, right? I know you . . . from a few classes we have . . . together," the girl said hesitantly.

"Yea, I am," I replied stiffly. The silence gave me the impression that she expected me to ask who she was, but I wasn't in the mood.

"Okay . . . .My name is Michaela," she said nervously. "I've been trying to get the courage to speak to you for a while now. I follow you on Twitter . . . I'm TDOTGIRL. I really admire the stuff you post," she said.

Michaela was one of the most beautiful girls I've met at Trinity. She had brown wavy tresses that fell to the middle of her back, appeared to be about 5 ft 5 inches and had big, wide, beautiful brown eyes.

"Thanks," I replied. "The only reason I have social media is to share what I know, you know? On stuff that isn't common knowledge but should be."

She nodded her head and laughed; a cute, shy chuckle.

"I'm sorry, did I make a joke?" I asked. I was used to being laughed at and I'm sure my look was killing her.

"No, no, please don't be offended. I just really admire you. I admire the way you live for a cause, you know? Your passion for equality is really, really . . . admirable." Michaela stuttered, looking down at her nude suede, strappy, chunky heeled sandals. The students at this school dressed like they attended New York Fashion Week.

"Well thanks, I really appreciate you noticing," I said.

Michaela hastily pulled out a piece of colourful paper from her white

Michael Kors tote bag. Fidgeting with the paper, she said. "Listen, Emily, I'll cut to the chase. I'm a photographer for the Oracle and our senior editor told us about a protest that will happen next Tuesday downtown on Yonge Street. You probably already know about it, but just in case, I thought I would share it with you. It's a Black People Unite rally to bring awareness to the fires erupting in vulnerable neighbourhoods these past few weeks. Black People Unite is a well-known group based in Toronto but has been gaining international recognition. Their overall aim is to speak out against injustices Black people face in Toronto and on a global scale. The group started around two years ago to combat the struggles faced by Black and Indigenous people within Canada."

"I know who they are," I said in an unintentionally snappy tone. I took the flyer from her hands and read it. If the newspaper team was told about this, why didn't Francis mention it? He knew all the ins and outs of this sort of thing.

"These injustices didn't just start happening Michaela. They have been happening for over 400 years." I retorted.

"Yes, sorry, of course. I know that. I really think you should come, though. There will be a lot of influencers there who will be speaking out about these Toronto housing fires. It's going to be a really outstanding event to highlight these deliberate fires."

Realizing this would not be a brief conversation and needing to conserve my headphone's battery for the bus journey home, I shut it off. "Who is in charge of this protest?" I asked.

"Uh, I'm not sure who actually coordinated the event, but it's worth checking it out."

"Uh-huh," I said as I scoped out the details on the flyer. "Thanks for letting me know," I said to Michaela. "I'll think about it."

"I really think you are someone who should attend this event," she continued.

I looked over at her. Her wide eyes and innocent expression made it hard to read her intentions. Was she really being nice to me, or was this another version of Katherine Caldwell trying to make me look stupid?

"What exactly is your motive here Michaela?" I asked her pointedly, turning to face her fully.

"What do you mean?"

"What I mean is, what are you gaining from promoting this event? Do you work with an advertising agency that pays you commission for every person you recruit? Who are these influencers who are attending? What are they getting out of it?"

Michaela looked dumbfounded at my questions. "Are you implying that because I'm white, I have to have an ulterior motive for promoting this event?"

I shrugged.

"Emily, I really don't think it's fair to judge someone you don't know based on their skin colour."

"I'm not judging you. I simply asked you two very . . . relevant questions." I said.

"The injustices against Black people affect me personally." She looked as if she was on the verge of tears, and suddenly I softened up.

"Okay," I said, letting up on the interrogation.

"Thank you for your time. I hope to see you there," she said stoically before walking away.

Just then, the bus arrived, only a mere fifteen minutes later. On the ride home, I found myself even more frustrated after the conversation with Michaela. I replayed it in my head and wondered why I automatically assumed that her intentions were impure. Clearly, I offended her with my implication. Why was I so defensive with her? And why didn't Francis tell me about this protest? Obviously, this is something I would be interested in, even this random girl knew it. I decided not to ruminate, at least for now.

Approaching my stop, I pulled down the yellow cord and hopped out of the bus. I walked to the beat of the music toward Francis' house. He was going to get a piece of my mind for leaving me at school. Storming up to his front door, I aggressively pressed down on the doorbell five times with my index finger. I waited for a few seconds but when I didn't hear any footsteps coming towards the door; I pressed my nose against the transparent glass to see if I could make out a silhouette . . . nothing. Angrily, I turned around and walked. I reached the concrete sidewalk before spinning around to face the house again. I stood there tapping my feet, trying to release my frustration. Just then, my phone vibrated, and with haste, I took it out of my pocket. But it wasn't a message from Francis, just social media notifications that I had no interest in. Deep in thought, I squeezed my phone like I was excreting juice from a lemon. Then I sent him a text.

I'm outside you clown, let me in!

I pushed my phone back in my pants pocket, waiting for a reply. I walked up to the door again and rang the doorbell incessantly until I could see a figure.

"I'm coming, I'm coming," the voice on the other side of the door said in an annoyed tone.

Blood rushed to my face in embarrassment. In all my anger and excitement, I had completely forgotten that Francis' mother could very well be home.

CHAPTER 7
WHAT DID SIS JUST SAY?!

Mrs. Porter opened the front door wearing a messy, stained white apron and her usual white dress shirt with black slacks. I looked down at her apron and read the bold red words stretched across her chest: Kiss me, I'm Mrs. Chef Porter.

"Hey Emily!" she sounded out of breath and looked a little dishevelled.

Ashamed by my antics, I twirled the end of a strand of my hair and replied shyly, "Hi Mrs. Porter, sorry about ringing your bell so many times. I just stopped by to see Francis."

"Oh, that's okay!" She cheered. "I was wondering who it was." She flicked a wooden mixing spoon in the air and as she spoke, a milky substance dripped off the spoon and onto the white marble floor in the foyer. "Francis isn't home yet," she said as she wiped off the spoon using her apron. "But you can come in and wait for him if you'd like."

He wasn't home yet? I thought. He left school before me . . . weh the backside this boy, d'eh?

"Ah, no, that's okay," I said, pulling out my phone and checking the time. "I'll just call him later."

"It's no trouble, Emily. Come on in. I'm sure he'll be home soon. I was just finishing up in the kitchen." She leaned against the door frame and pushed the door wide open, just enough for the both of us to stand in the doorway. I studied her face; she looked as if she'd been crying.

When she caught me staring at her, Mrs. Porter stood to the side and awkwardly motioned for me to walk inside. Reluctantly, I entered.

"I just took a Shepherd's pie out of the oven. Would you like a slice?" She offered politely as she led me into the kitchen. Her high, messy ponytail swished from side to side as she turned her head periodically to check if I was still behind her.

I took off my ballet flats and opened the white front closet door as she continued towards the kitchen. Mrs. Porter was impeccably organized, and she arranged her closet according to colour and shades of fur coats. I looked meticulously for an appropriate spot to place mine.

As if reading my mind, Mrs. Porter's distanced voice said, "Just put them with the blacks, Emily. There should be a space at the front."

I did as I was told and made my way to the kitchen with my schoolbag on my shoulder. There, in the middle of the marble island, sat a matte white baking dish. Inside of the dish lay a pie made from potatoes. I'd seen shepherd's pie in the cafeteria at school many times, but I wasn't interested in trying it. Beside the dish lay two huge photo albums. They were both open, and she sprawled photos all over the surface. Deep red wine droplets coated a cute picture of Francis in diapers.

"Oh no thank you, Mrs. Porter. I'm okay," I replied with a shy smile. I prayed that this woman would not force this food on me.

"Oh nonsense," she insisted. "Have a seat on one of the bar stools and I'll cut you a slice."

As I sat down, she took a sip of her wine and picked up a stainless steel knife from a fancy silver holder.

"Would you like a glass of wine?" she asked as she turned around, exposing a sly smile on her face. "I'm just kidding!" she said laughing and tapping on the counter. Her laugh reminded me of Ursula from *The Little Mermaid*.

I chuckled uncomfortably.

Placing a glass plate in front of me. The piece of shepherd's pie looked more like a brick. Laying in all its glory was a huge chunk of the ground beef and mashed potatoes layered into a concoction. She then handed me a soft white cloth napkin that was neatly wrapped around a silver knife and fork set inside.

"Water, milk, or apple juice, love?" she asked enthusiastically.

"Water is fine, thank you," I replied. I placed the cutlery on the right of the glass plate.

Handing me a crystal glass of iced water, she stood on the other side of the island, directly facing me. "You know, Emily, you and I have never really had time to talk … woman to woman." She dragged one album closer to her and started flipping through it.

I unfolded the napkin and stuck the fork into the shepherd's pie. Now it looked like a flagpole stuck in solid stone. Picking up a tiny piece, I put it in my mouth. Chewing slowly and cautiously, I listened to her go on. She put the glass of wine to her mouth, finished the remains and poured herself another full glass from the bottle that read, "Kim Crawford Merlot."

"Is there anything specific that you would like to talk about, Mrs. Porter?" I guessed she probably wanted to tell me politely that she was uncomfortable with me dating her son, since everyone and their mother thought we were dating.

"Did Francis ever tell you about his dad?" she asked.

But wait, a nuh this mi did a expect! I thought to myself, trying to hide my astonishment. Sipping the ice-cold water to aid in swallowing a piece of mushy potato pie, I replied through a mouthful, "He only told me you and his dad got divorced when he was eight, nothing more." Again, I picked up my glass of water to buy myself some more time from eating the meal.

"Hmm," she said as she swished her wine glass around and gazed outside. She was deep in concentration. "Francis' father was my first love," she began. "We met in high school. I was seventeen, grade eleven at Trinity, and he was eighteen, in grade twelve."

I picked at the shepherd's pie as I listened uncomfortably, yet intently, to the random story.

She continued as she stared into space. "I was madly in love with him. On our first date, do you know where we went?" she asked me.

I hunched over, clasped my hands, and placed them in between my thighs.

"Oh, no! Are you cold?" she asked shockingly, "Oh let me turn up the thermostat!"

Before I could let her know that the shift in my bodily position was because of her drunk ranting and not from being cold, she ran up to the thermostat and began experimenting with it. I watched in awe as her left finger stayed fixed on a button and in her right hand; she brought the glass to her lips, chugging the wine like it was juice. "I can't change the temperature!" she screamed in a whiny toddler voice. "They jumble all the words and numbers."

It was clear Mrs. Porter started drinking before I got there.

Suddenly, she began laughing hysterically and gave up on how "cold" the house was. Making her way over to me... or maybe it was back to her albums, she sauntered over in my direction and tripped over her slippers, dropping her wine glass shattering on the fancy light grey marble tile. "NOO," she screamed. It all seemed like slow motion, but this was no movie. She collapsed to the floor dramatically and sat in the puddle of wine and glass. "That was one of my wedding wine glasses!" she screamed and started bawling, living eye water.

I sat there for a few seconds, wondering what on earth I was supposed to do. *Really . . . I should just leave this mess of a woman here and go about my business, but how often does this type of opportunity arise where I can actually know what happened between her and Francis' dad?* I rushed over to her and helped her up. "Come on, Mrs. Porter, this is not like you," I said as gently as I could.

She stood up, and we trudged to the stool beside the one I was sitting on.

She plopped down on it and her ponytail dropped in front of her face, blocking her eyes from the world. "You're so right, Emily, this isn't me," she said, looking up at me with soaked eyes and nodding profusely. "I used to have the marriage that all my girlfriends envied. Now look at me, here day drunk and pining over a pathetic man who left me for a black woman!"

Woah! What did sis just say? My jaw literally dropped. Quickly, I turned my head away from her to hide the "you've got to be kidding me" expression that crept across my face. When I collected myself, I said, "Mrs. Porter, it's going to be alright. Come on, let me help you to the bathroom so you can wash your face. You're all red and puffy now."

She used what looked like all her energy to get up, but the poor thing could only stand for a second. Losing patience, I said sternly, "Mrs. Porter, help me, help you. I can't lift you up. Now come, on the count of three."

"I can't make it to the powder room, Emily, it's too far," she said through slurred words.

"Okay then, let's go to the kitchen sink," I said.

"That is an incredible idea!" she yelled. "You're such a smart girl, that's why my son loves you sooo much." She lifted her head and gave me a wide smile.

I Ignored her comment. "One, two, three," I counted, and she garnered the courage to stand somewhat firmly. She put her left hand around my shoulders and we slowly made our way to the kitchen sink that was directly behind the island. Hunched over the sink, she tried to find the pipe to no avail. I helped homegirl out by pulling the lever. The water rushed out of the pipe so aggressively it sounded like strong winds blowing. Her pale, perfectly manicured hands dangled under the pipe, water bouncing off her sparkly nails.

"Mrs. Porter, please wash your face," I begged.

"Okay, okay," she said. Slowly but surely, she wet her face over and over until she came back to life. After a few minutes of washing, she said "I'm done" and I handed her a piece of paper towel. She patted her face dry and sighed. "I thought he and I would be together forever, Emily," she continued.

Yes, yes, go on.

"Then one day," she paused, grabbed the album from off the island and took out a picture of a tall, muscular David Beckham look alike. Waving it frantically at me, she said, "Then one night, he came home and told me he was leaving me for this black girl with three kids. It literally came out of nowhere. He just handed me the divorce papers, packed up his things, kissed Francis as he slept, and left."

I just stared at her with a pitiful look on my face. I truly had no words, and it was rare that I was left speechless.

"Do you know where he took me on our first date?" she repeated. She looked at me as if waiting for an answer.

"No?" I said with a simple neck roll. *How would I know? What's wrong with sis?*

"He took me to a private drive-In movie that he planned himself. We watched Casablanca, my favourite film. He told me he would love no one else the way he loved me." She started crying again, loudly this time.

I handed her another piece of paper towel.

"I just wish I could get some closure," she said through sniffles.

"Closure?" I prompted.

She came close to my face as if she was studying every pore and feature. "I just need to know why. Why her? How could he leave me for a woman like her?"

My eyes grew large, *what did she mean by 'a woman like her'?"*

I was both intrigued and uncomfortable. "I'm very sorry to hear that, Mrs. Porter, and I appreciate you sharing this with me, but I really have to get going. Please let Francis know I stopped by," I said as I grabbed my backpack and attempted to leave.

"Wait, let me pack this up for you," she said as she stood up and tried to smooth the crumples out of her apron. She grabbed a Pyrex container from her cupboard above the sink.

"Oh, really, you don't have to. Does that travel well?"

"Don't worry about it. Just pop it in the microwave when you get home and it'll be good to go." She handed me the container. Unwillingly, I took it and put it in my bag.

As she walked me to the door, she said, "Emily, I'm really sorry you had to see me like this. I hope it doesn't change your perception of me."

"No, no, Mrs. Porter, no judgement here," I lied.

She smiled, and we said our goodbyes.

I did the fifteen-minute walk instead of taking the bus that would be a five-minute ride home. I needed to dissect all the happenings of today. No music, just my thoughts and me.

First, where was Francis? I checked my phone, and I realized that not only did he not reply to my text; the message did not deliver. *Did he get kidnapped? Why was he being so sketchy? What was that situation I just experienced with Mrs. Perfect Porter? No wonder Francis never let me talk to his mother for too long. He clearly didn't want me to know the details regarding his father. But why? He and I were supposed to be best friends. Why would he keep this a secret? Was he ashamed? Why would he be ashamed? He and I have told each other more intimate stuff than this. This is boggling my mind.*

I unlocked my front door and went into the kitchen. I dumped the Shepherd's pie into the compost, washed the Pyrex container and dried it with a paper towel. I was glad to dispose of it before my mother came home and saw it. She would have definitely had a fit. If there is one thing she hates, it's eating from other people. I went to my room, Pyrex in hand, and flopped down on the chair around my desk. I put the container in my bag, determined to return it to the owner tomorrow. Taking a sip of water from my Contigo metal water bottle, I opened my journal.

September 20, 2016 3:35pm,

I had the most bizarre day. I'm not even sure where to begin.

I'm pretty sure Francis hates me. He didn't say it, but when he read my article, I felt it. That weird thing he does when he has a problem with me. He doesn't say it, he just clams up.

I ended up submitting my second piece to the "Oracle". My mother and Francis said the first one was horrible. Francis, like my mom, tore my article to shreds on the bus this morning while we were on our way to school. But now I think submitting the second piece was the worst thing I could have done. I wish I had followed my gut. I know the original piece was better.

THEN TO TOP IT ALL OFF, Mrs. Porter was pissed drunk today. She told me something I knew absolutely nothing about. She told me that Francis's dad left her and Francis for a black woman with three kids.

Is this why Mrs. Porter is so obsessed with Black people and culture? Is she trying to overcompensate for something? I sensed a vibe from the way she told the story. To say it was a blow to her ego is an understatement. Sis was like: He left me for a Black woman! Blasphemy in my eyes!

All that aside, though, I really wonder why Francis did not tell me about this. I thought he and I had a close and honest friendship, but how can I trust someone who keeps selective secrets for absolutely no reason . . .

I closed my journal and placed it in my backpack. I was done journaling for the day. I got up, put my hair in a messy bun, and went into the shower. I needed to wash the confusing day off of me. As I stripped down in front of the mirror and turned on the scalding water, I thought to myself, my plan for the night? Brush my teeth, wash my face and jump into bed. No dinner tonight . . . I think that pie made me sick.

CHAPTER 8

BLANK SLATE

I woke up to the sad realization that it was only Tuesday and still no texts from Francis. Fighting the urge to text him again, I got out of bed to begin my morning ritual. I took a quick shower in silence. My mind was still reeling from the awkward encounter with Mrs. Porter. I just wanted a clear headspace to think, while I slathered my body with my favourite body wash.

Visions of Mrs. Porter's wide drunken smile came rushing back to me like the water beating down on my shoulders from the rainstorm shower head. Shaking it off, I closed my eyes tight, trying to think about something else. *You're such a smart girl, that's why my son loves you sooo much.*

Anxious thoughts fired questions off in my mind. *If he "loves me" so much, why is he ignoring me . . . yea, right?*

After drying my body off, I rifled through the drawer of uniform variations among heavy, exhausted grunts. Reluctantly, I grabbed a matching navy blue underwear set from my drawer then slid the white, wooden panelled closet open to take my neatly ironed khaki pants and long sleeve golf shirt off the hanger. Fully clothed, I made my way back into my bathroom and squirted a small amount of my olive, avocado, and Jamaican black castor oil mixture into my palms. Unravelling my six jumbo twists, I used a black plastic hair pick to fluff the curls. The last touch was a satin navy headband and a pair of silver hoop earrings. Taking one more glance in the mirror, I applied a thin layer of NYX soft matte lip cream in the shade "Monte Carlo." The deep cranberry red complimented my skin perfectly.

"Done," I said, looking into the mirror. Then I grabbed my backpack from the foot of my desk and rushed down the stairs.

On the bus, I drank a smoothie slowly, preventing any spills from landing on my uniform. My attempt at making myself busy and forgetting the happenings for yesterday proved unsuccessful as I saw Francis hopping onto the bus. Pretending not to see him, I stared out the window.

"Hey," he said to me softly, sitting down in the seat beside me. His voice sounded raspy, as if he had been screaming at a music festival all night.

I pretended not to notice. "Hey," I replied, still staring out the window.

"My mom said you stopped by yesterday looking for me . . . were you there long?"

"Nope," I replied, and took a sip of my smoothie.

"Oh," He replied. "That's weird. My mom said that you came in and had some Shepherd's pie."

Changing my gaze from the moving trees and buildings outside, I turned my head and looked at him. "In all the years that you have known me, have you ever heard me express any interest in eating Shepherd's pie?" I asked.

Francis laughed, "No, I haven't."

I returned to the window, and it was silent for a minute before he continued.

"So . . . did you guys, like, hang out or . . . ?"

Under normal circumstances, I would've taken this opportunity to tell him the truth and have a deep heart-to-heart conversation with my friend. On a normal day, Francis would've probably opened up about his family hardship, after probing, and I would've offered a supportive shoulder for him to cry on, but based on how he was acting, I felt like playing the same game as him. *I'll play aloof.* "Honestly, we didn't talk about much. She invited me in, asked me how my day at school was, and I waited a bit for you. When you didn't show, I left."

He started twiddling his thumbs as we sat on the moving bus in silence.

"So where were you?" I said sharply, cutting the silence with my harsh tone.

"I was just at the park. I wasn't feeling well and just needed a break from socializing, so I went to the park to write some poetry," he replied.

That response was a no for me. I didn't buy it one bit. "And you couldn't have told me you just needed time to yourself? I rushed to submit my paper because I didn't want you to wait for me."

His phone screen lit up, and he stuffed it away in his bag, quickly.

"Emily, please, just drop it. I really don't even see what the big deal is. So you had to bus home by yourself. You know the way. I wasn't feeling well, and I needed a break from you. Why can't you just understand that? Everything is not about you all the time."

"Wow." I chuckled at his lame attempt to flip the script. The Toronto transit bus slowed down as it approached Trinity. I stood up and mumbled, "Excuse me please" while pushing Francis' legs out of my way.

I didn't want to admit it, but those words pierced me like a knife.

"I need a break from *you*," I repeated to myself as I walked to the bus's exit door. Francis followed. Waiting for the doors to open, he stood directly behind me and his warm breath pressed against the back of my neck. In this small space crowded with students, I felt my anxiety rise. His breath crawled up my neck as if he was getting closer to whisper something in my ear. Then the door flew open, and I stormed out.

Tunnel vision forming, I hastened toward my locker.

"Emily, wait!"

I heard Francis' faint voice behind me, so I quickened my pace.

"Emily, can you please wait?"

I heard him again, but kept walking.

When Francis finally caught up to me, he grabbed my shoulders with both hands and turned my body to face him.

"Look, I'm sorry I snapped at you," he said, his hands gripping my slim shoulders.

"It's fine," I said and turned to continue walking. He didn't stop me this time.

"Good luck today . . . I hope you get on the newspaper team!" he yelled.

"Yea, thanks," I yelled back. Tunnel vision still in effect.

I arrived at my first-period class ten minutes early and quickly took my seat in the middle right corner. With so many thoughts running around in my head, I sneaked a quick journaling session in before everyone else arrived for English.

Tuesday, September 21, 2016. 8:10 am

Francis is acting so shady. He's lying to me and keeping secrets from me as well. What is that about? What did I do? I haven't even been able to think much about the newspaper team. Maybe it's nerves. I wanted to confide in Francis about it, but he made himself so scarce yesterday and today he was being evasive. When he needs me, I'm there. When I need him . . . well . . . that's a different story.

I just want to be chosen . . . by the newspaper team and . . . others. I feel like this is my last chance to make friends here. I'm pretty sure this is the only place that I could fit in at Trinity. How else will I be able to survive the remaining years in this school?

Just then, my writing was interrupted by the voice of a tall, slender middle-aged man carrying a black leather briefcase. He had jet black shiny hair and pearly white teeth.

"Good Morning everyone. My name is Mr. Robertson and I will be your supply teacher for the month, as Mrs. Pratt is absent."

The class ignored his announcement and remained glued to their phones. The 24 inch LED TV screen in each classroom lit up and the daily announcements began. *Talk about a developed nation.* As advanced as my previous school was in Jamaica, there were definitely no televisions in each classroom. My classmates and I stood as "Oh Canada" played over the PA system. When it finally ended, we all sat down and two students from the senior class appeared on the screen to give the news for the day.

"Happy Tuesday, everyone! I hope you're having a glorious morning!" The first student, a brunette with long straight hair and plumped red lips, said.

"Let's dive right into the announcements!" The other student chimed in. He was a bleach blond-haired boy wearing lots of hair gel.

"First up, announcements about the newspaper team! As you know, two weeks ago, the newspaper editor, Angelique James and the overseer, Mr. Chow, asked for submissions from interested candidates hoping to join this year's award-winning newspaper team, the Trinity Oracle. The assignment was to submit a short literary piece of your choice. Well, the team has made their decision on who will join the team for the rest of the school year."

I looked around the class; it seemed as if I was the only person who cared about the announcements. While I glued my eyes to the screen, everyone around me was in full chatter mode. I extended my ears so I could hear the tv above the noise.

"We will now turn the mic over to Angelique, The Oracle's editor."

"Thank you, Amy," Angelique said, appearing on the screen. At face value, Angelique reminded me of a Disney star. Do you know that popular high school girl in the movies? She gave me that vibe and emulated the character of the perfect blonde, blue-eyed girl adored by everyone. Not me, but everyone else.

"I would like to start off by thanking and congratulating everyone who tried out for the newspaper team," Angelique said. "With that said, we received a lot of submissions and they were all incredible."

Okay, Angelique, get to it. I tapped my pen lightly on the wooden desk.

"Unfortunately, we can only accept four people this year. Those four are Francis Porter in grade 10, Molly Nilsson in grade 11, Katherine Caldwell in grade 10 and our very own, Emily . . . McMaster in grade 12."

McMaster. Not Morrison. McMaster. I repeated in my mind. It was safe to say; this crushed me.

***

The rest of the school day moved along slowly, as if it was taunting me for not getting chosen for the thing I wanted most here.

As I sat in fourth period history, I anxiously waited for the day to end. I loved history. It was actually my favourite subject, but I was just so ready to go home. As the teacher droned on and on about the Roman empire, I thought about just calling it a day and heading home.

Why did I think I was going to make the newspaper? I really fooled myself. So much for calling my classmates to action. I moaned internally.

I checked my phone periodically as I waited for the day to end. Not one text from Francis. He didn't even have the decency to send me a fake sympathetic text . . . he was probably celebrating. I sent him a text, even though I was still mad at him.

Congrats, Francis . . .

Hours later, still no reply.

In my mind, I could hear him say, "I told you the piece was too controversial." Without a doubt, he would blame me for not being selected for the team without even knowing that the piece I had submitted was not the one he read. I decided I wouldn't reach out to him for the rest of the day. That would set us up for another fight. Instead, I sent a text to my father.

Hey, can you pick me up from school at 2:30pm?

Sure. Are you okay?

Yea, I'm fine. I just don't feel like taking the bus home.

Okay, I'll see you at 2:30pm sharp, Boops.

I sent a thumbs up emoji and a smiley face, even though I wanted to crumble into a ball and cry.

At 2:30pm, I ran to my locker to switch my history book to my English book to prepare for a quiz. My locker door was nearly off its hinges. Aiming to meet my dad on time, I grabbed all the contents of my locker and poured it all into my bag. I would leave nothing in here until the damn school fixed it. I hurried because my dad had a lot of exceptional qualities, but patience was not one of them. Exiting the building, my dad's car pulled into the school parking lot. He slowed down and came to a stop as I hopped in the pearl white 2016 Honda Civic Coupe.

"Hey daddy, thanks for picking me up," I said.

"Yeah man, you good, Boops?" he replied. He put the car in park and turned slightly to face me, his chocolate skin glistening against the sun.

"Something is wrong. Are you okay?" he asked.

"Yes dad, I'm fine," I laughed nervously.

"Don't lie to me, Emily. What's wrong?"

After releasing a heavy sigh, I said, "I didn't make the newspaper team."

The sound of a loud car horn interrupted our conversation. We both turned around in sync and realized that my dad was actually blocking the exit of the school without realizing it. Quickly, he reversed the sports car into the nearest parking space and cracked his door to apologize.

"Sorry about that."

We watched as an angry brunette wound her window down and shouted expletives at us with her daughter, a schoolmate of mine, in the front seat. "What's wrong with you?" she screamed. "Didn't they teach you how to drive in Africa?" The teen in the back laughed and pulled her iPhone out to record.

Like a knee-jerk reaction, I wound my window down and pushed my head out aggressively. At the top of my lungs, I screamed and pointed at her, "Racist witch!"

"Emily!" my dad yelled. "Put your head back inna d car! Weh yuh a do?"

"What do you mean, what am I doing?" I asked, annoyed.

Suddenly, the heat was emerging from inside my body and onto the surface as beads of sweat. I put my hair up and took my hoops out. "We can't let her speak to us like that," I said. I flung open the door, ready for a fight with the ole gyal, but she jammed down on her gas, turned right and sped off down the street. At that moment, I wished I was driving my own car.

"Emily, learn to have thick skin and ignore ignorant people."

I was fuming at the fact that this lady had the nerve to say what she said and that my dad sat there defending her. Getting back into the car and closing the passenger door, I said, "Please daddy, let's just go home."

"Before we leave," he said, "I want to tell you . . . I know you're disappointed about not making the newspaper team, but please don't be discouraged. You can always try again next year."

"I'm not trying again," I snapped with my arms folded.

"Which piece did you submit?" he asked softly, as he wiped a fallen tear away from my cheek.

"I submitted the second piece I wrote," I replied.

He was silent for a few seconds, then he said, "What was it about?"

"Dad, please, I don't want to talk about this anymore," I said. "Let's just go home."

CHAPTER 9

CURRIED SHRIMP

Moments later, my father turned into the paved driveway of our house and put the car in park. I opened the door before he could even turn off the engine.

"What do you want for dinner?" he asked.

"Not hungry," I said firmly. He shot me a surprised look, and I knew where this was headed.

"Nope, we na do dat. You affi eat something. If I follow you, you'll sit there and starve and then yuh madda a g'uh blame me for your starvation." He was trying to make me laugh, but it didn't work.

"But I'm not hungry," I repeated as we walked up to the front door.

He gave me a big, tight squeeze and said, "I'll make some curried shrimp and white rice. How dat soun'?" He knew I wouldn't be able to resist my favourite meal.

I laughed, "Sounds great, dad," I said, feigning for some happiness.

To be honest, I was actually looking forward to that dish. He didn't make it often, but when he did, I loved it. Dad opened the door, and I passed by him and climbed upstairs to my room. As usual, the first thing I did was drop my school bag at the foot of my desk. Then I went into the bathroom accompanied by my iPhone. I was in mid-pee and scrolling on Instagram when a message from Francis popped up on my screen. I opened it.

I'm sorry you didn't make the team.

It's cool.

He read the message. Two minutes later he sent . . .

I hate to say it, but I told you so. You shouldn't have submitted such a
controversial piece.

If you really hated to say it, you wouldn't have said it, Francis.

Three dots popped up and disappeared.

Before you even go any further, let me just tell you. I am not in the mood
for this. Spare me your bs . . .

He read the message. The three grey dots appeared and disappeared again.

I'm not trying to make you upset, but I wouldn't be true to myself if I didn't let you know. If I were you, I would take this as a lesson. Now you know, maybe it isn't the smartest thing to write about kids at Trinity or such heavy topics, especially for a school newspaper. You are a decent writer, but you're too focused on issues surrounding race and it is hindering your achievement.

At his last statement, I locked my phone and placed it on my bathroom sink countertop as I washed my hands.

"Yup, I think I'm done for the day," I said to myself before taking off my clothes and turning the shower on. After a few minutes, the water was at the right temperature. I was about to step in when my phone started vibrating.

"Francis Porter" covered the entire screen. Below his name, I had two options: answer and decline.

I pressed decline.

After my quick shower, I covered myself with body butter and ran downstairs, where I was greeted by the heavenly smell of West Indian curry. Even after the worst day in history, the smell of homemade meals makes everything better. There's something about my dad's cooking that brings so much joy to my heart. Maybe it's the way he dances as he expertly burns the curry before adding the seasoning and the shrimp. Maybe it's the way he delicately prepares and plates the meal. But when I smell the sweet aroma of his chef skills and hear the fan over the stove blow away the steam from the pan, I always laugh to myself, thinking: This man only knows how to cook with the burner on high.

I eagerly sat on the middle bar stool waiting to be served my favourite dinner. "I am so excited about this, daddy, thank you!" I said through a wide grin.

"You're welcome, Boops," he replied as he placed the colourful plate in front of me. He delicately sprinkled the curried gravy over the rice, just the way I liked it, and he plated sauteed spinach, the only vegetable I like. My dad and I ate and chatted about our day.

"So, I've been applying for jobs again." He told me he spent most of the day doing it. "Your mom keeps begging me to network with some parents on the Trinity list." My dad was referring to the "networking," list the school gave out every year to parents. "Em, I'm so unhappy in this job, and I'm butting heads with this new manager. It's affecting my performance at work."

"Dad, just because mom networked her way to a better job, with that list, doesn't mean you have to," I mentioned.

"I know . . ." his voice trailed off. "Being here, it's like we have to keep up with the other families . . . your mom seems to like the competition but I just can't get into it."

I knew how he felt. My dad and I still felt like outsiders in Toronto. Between bites, I wondered if we'd ever feel at home here.

As he swallowed his last bite, he asked me, "When was the last time you spoke to your grandma?"

"Two and a half weeks . . . maybe," I spoke through a full mouthful of rice.

"You should probably call her," he said as he sucked the curried gravy from the tail of the shrimp. "I'm sure she'll give you the pep talk you need right now."

He had a point there.

DING! Just then, my iPhone chimed four times in a row. I unlocked my phone and the conversation thread appeared.

I have the perfect pick-me-up! Let's blow off some steam. Let's go to Willies! I'll get my mom to drive us.

My dad made dinner. Go without me. Plus, I have to study for my English quiz.

Oh, okay. Let's go tomorrow after school then.

K.

I placed the phone upside down on the table and finished my last bit of rice. Maybe this was his attempt to bury the hatchet and finally get back to being normal friends again . . . normal . . . were we ever normal, to begin with?

CHAPTER 10

SWEET DUMPLING

My phone buzzed against the wooden end table next to my bed. When it rang, my body jolted upright while my eyes adjusted to the blue light emanating from the glass iPhone screen.

In the darkness of my bedroom, I searched for the time. It was 2am and an unknown caller was waking me up.

"Hello?" My voice croaked. But before I could ask who it was, a smooth Caribbean accent flowed through the receiver's end.

"I ave yuh money."

My eyes shot open. Shocked at the sound of the familiar voice, she continued speaking.

"Listen, I ave yuh money. I'm paying you back for the hotel room." The voice continued after a moment of silence. "Yuh go to that private school downtown with the uniforms, right?"

"Uh, yes. Yes, I do . . . it's called Trinity Collegiate." I answered.

"Okay, I will drop off an envelope with the money to the office." It was quiet once again. Her voice was low, almost a whisper.

"What's your name?" I said, sitting up now, resting my back against the headboard of my bed.

A moment of silence sat between us as if she was contemplating. "I can't . . . I can't talk long here, you've helped me enough." In the background, I could hear a muffled voice urging her off the phone.

"You don't have to–" I said, but in an instant, the line went dead. The phone cut off and suddenly she was gone again.

A few hours later, I sat down at my desk, getting ready for school. Going back to sleep after that phone call was impossible, so I stayed up all night journalling. While I sat on my desk chair, taking in my surroundings, I realized how lucky I was to live so comfortably in Canada. Sure, things weren't always so easy. When we first arrived, we lived in a one-bedroom basement apartment before drifting into an apartment building in Etobicoke. When I started at Trinity, my mom networked her way towards owning a huge brownstone in Hillel Gardens. These were the stories Francis never heard about. He wouldn't be able to understand those experiences, anyway. That was the thing. The thing that made me identify with the woman from the fire. Every day when I enter through those doors at school, I am reminded that I am an outsider who is infiltrating a foreign space. I may exist here, but other than that, I'm pretty much invisible, like her.

When we left Jamaica, it was at the height of robberies taking place in Clarendon. My parents just finished building their home, my mother's dream home, when we packed up and moved to Canada. We lived in that house for exactly six months. I guess my parents became tired of dealing with the extortionists who would show up every few months demanding to be paid for the work they weren't doing, or the thieves who would break into our house, somehow get passed the gate and the grill, smash our new French windows and rob us.

Now tenants are living there and paying rent. Now a little eight-year-old girl is growing up in the room that I decorated just for me. So I can't relate to the cottage stories, the celebrity gossip fests, or the hockey tales. Instead, I'm dismissed as the weird Jamaican girl who's always angry, a role I've learned to play well.

In the morning, I added layers of mascara to my eyelashes and attempted to call my grandmother before leaving for school.

"Hello good morning," a soft, polite and angelic Jamaican voice spoke up on the other end of the line.

"Hi Grandma, it's me, Emily."

"Oh Em Em, mi granddaughter, how are you doing?"

"I'm doing well, Grandma. How are you?" A standard answer.

"Blessed and highly favoured my child, blessed and highly favoured," she replied. My grandmother is always blessed and highly favoured. "So what's new, my sweet dumpling?" she asked cheerily.

I could have fibbed and said, "Nothing is new", but there's something about a conversation with my grandmother that makes me want to come clean. I let out a deep sigh. "Are you at work right now, grandma?" I asked, stalling. I didn't know where to begin.

"Yes, I am darling, but nuh worry 'bout that mi love, dem a g'waan without mi," she said in the Jamaican dialect, patois. That meant don't worry about my work, my love, because I certainly don't. My grandmother has always had the strongest personality, so I was confident that the interruption didn't bother her.

My grandmother, Ann-Marie Richardson, was a certified psychologist, and a well respected one at that. She worked for "the man" as she termed it for ten years until she decided she couldn't be enslaved any longer and opened her own practice. That was twenty years ago. What she loved most about being her own boss, as she liked to tell it, is that she didn't have to depend on anyone, especially someone who once owned our ancestors.

I asked her why she pursued psychology and she said, "It's because the mind of the racist intrigues me. I want to understand why they are the way they are." I also asked if she had encountered any racist patients in Jamaica.

She responded, "Jamaica's problem isn't direct racism so much as it is colourism and classism." She told me, "Colourism, Emily, stems from racism. It's the belief that people of lighter complexions and looser hair patterns are superior to people like you and me, dark, deeply melanated coloured skin, with coily hair. I've had many patients who were colourists and some who have been carrying around the baggage of being raised by colourist parents. I have had to unravel and undo a lot of hurt and negative thoughts that my clients had about themselves."

"Why does colourism exist grandma?" I once asked her.

"Colourism, my love, exists because of slavery. It's the baby of racism, but don't be fooled. It's just as tragic, heart-breaking and immoral. Remember what I told you?

"They hate us because they fear us," was my reply. It was always a pop quiz with my grandma. My grandmother always attempted to teach me about my history.

"A person who does not know where they came from can't know where they are going," she said to me, and that quote has been with me ever since.

In response to another deep sigh, my grandmother said in a worried tone, "Emily, what's the matter?"

"I don't know where to begin, grandma," I said.

"Begin at the beginning, child."

I started, "Okay, I tried out for the newspaper team, but I didn't make it."

"Now, now, Emily, you know the drill. In order for us to dissect the situation properly, I will need the complete story," she said sternly.

I sighed. It's serious when she gets into psychologist mode and starts treating me as one of her patients.

"I am not only hurt that I didn't make the team, but mad at myself because I wrote a great article and then I let Francis and mom talk me into submitting a different piece. I really think I could have made it if I followed my gut and submitted the first piece I wrote."

"Huh, I see," my grandmother replied, a usual response whenever her mind works at a rapid pace. "So sweetness, why do you think you didn't follow your gut?"

"I don't know," I lied.

"Come on now, Emily, a mi dis, why didn't you follow your gut?"

Reluctantly, I answered, "Because people said the first piece was too controversial, so I wrote a safer piece and submitted that instead."

"Hmm," she breathed.

"I know, I know, mi mus' always follow mi gut. I know grandma."

"So then, baby, if you know, why didn't you do it? Why did you let people get inside your head?"

"I don't know," I mumbled

"Okay, listen, I don't want you to cry over spilt milk. We both know you are an excellent writer. So you didn't make this team? You can try again, or you can search for writing groups in your area. Why don't you go ask them for feedback so you know where to improve? Tell you what, I will do a quick search on the Google and send you an email with what I find. How does that sound?"

"It sounds great, grandma, thank you," I said through an exhale. My shoulders fell in relief.

"What else is wrong?" grandma asked, concern still clouded her melodious tone.

"Why do you think something else is wrong?" I asked coyly.

"Likkle girl, stop di foolishness and doe m'ek mi get miserable pa you," she said jokingly.

I released a weak yet sincere laugh. "Arite, arite," I replied. "Well," I said slowly, calculating my thoughts to make sure I had all the information to tell her. "Your daughter and her husband are still fighting, almost every day. They're ignoring each other right now, and it's so annoying. Most times I just put my headphones in so I don't have to hear them fight." Now the floodgates were open and suddenly word vomit rushed out of my mouth, "and also I'm realizing now you were right about Francis. He's been sneaky lately."

My grandmother stayed silent and allowed me to continue.

"He's just being such a weirdo, mi nuh know wah happen to him." I was going to tell her about the woman from the fire, but decided not to.

"Wow, arite so you just said a lot, so give me a few seconds to play this all over again in my head," grandma said. My grandmother is blunt. A few seconds passed and then she said, "Before I say anything about what you've told me, just know seh, I am coming up there ASAP because a bere foolishness a g'waan and you obviously need me there."

Joy flooded my bloodstream. She was so right; I needed her here.

She continued, "I will say nothing about this Francis person, except you already know I don't like him as a friend for you. But regarding this not believing in yourself thing, you know I have always encouraged you to show up and support matters you believe in. That is what activism is about."

"Yes," I said, point-blank.

"Then go, please be yourself from now on, don't let the words of likkle kids bring you down. You have important things to say." She warned. "And regarding your parents. Keep putting your headphones on and drowning them out. I am coming up here to sort them out, so don't even stress about that. Your job is to be a child and get excellent grades. I know how your mother can be and I just hope she isn't stressing out poor Frank too much."

I heard her office door creak open.

"Darling, my next patient has arrived." She whispered into the phone.

I whispered an "I love you" and hung up. I always missed her even more after a phone conversation, but knowing that she would be here soon made me thrilled.

***

Francis met me at the bus stop after school the next day and we went to Willie's Diner, the local hangout spot for Trinity kids. It was about fifteen minutes away from the school. Everyone went to Willies on Fridays to celebrate the weekend, but Francis mentioned on the bus that today was a special occasion and I needed to "unwind and forget about the newspaper." We sat down on the blood-red leather seats in a secluded booth at the back of the restaurant and waited for a server to come to us.

After a few minutes, Francis said, "We really should have known better than to sit down and wait for a server." The booth fabric made its usual fart sound as he got up. He turned to face me and asked, "The usual, right?"

I nodded, "Yep. Thanks."

While he went to order two loaded burgers, sweet potato fries and a side of mayo and vinegar for me, my fingers glided down my phone screen as I viewed my Twitter timeline absentmindedly. Apart from a few retweets, my tweet about the woman from the fire fell on deaf ears. I interrupted my scrolling when three teens standing on the performance stage in the middle of the diner caught my attention. I recognized Michaela as one of them, and she held a megaphone to her bright pink lips.

"Hey everyone, can I just interrupt for a quick sec?" she yelled. "I just want to remind you guys that The Black People Unite protest is tomorrow at Yonge and Dundas." She said, her soft voice now booming throughout the restaurant. "With the recent Toronto housing fires, many marginalized families are out on the streets tonight. Shelters are filling up quickly, our generation needs to get serious about righting the wrongs of society. Specifically, regarding the injustice our Black and Indigenous brothers and sisters have faced." She continued while the restaurant flowed at its busy pace.

Servers were still taking orders and guests were having their very important conversations amongst themselves. She stepped down, and everyone returned to regular programming. Not even a pitiful "woot" was heard.

Wow, how great it was to be a millennial. I shook my head. Who was going to this thing, anyway? I pulled up the event on Facebook, "Black People Unite Toronto Chapter." I clicked the "see all" link to see who had RSVP'd.

"Hey Emily," Michaela said, approaching my booth with her megaphone in hand.

"Hi, how are you?" I asked.

"Fine, thanks. Can I sit down?"

"Yea, sure," I offered, and scooted over to give her space to sit. "Hey, listen, I'm sorry if I came across as rude the other day when I met you. I was in a really foul mood," I confessed as she sat down.

"It's cool. If it upset me, I wouldn't have come over to you now." She laughed, fiddling with the megaphone in both hands.

"True," I said. "So what's up?" I smiled.

"Are you going to the protest?" she asked.

"I don't know yet, maybe."

She placed the megaphone at her feet, then looked up to face me. "You really should," she said as she put her long, flowing hair in a ponytail. "I saw your tweet about Miss Yvette Ivy Williams."

I looked at her, confused. "Miss Ivy who?"

"The woman in the article you tweeted." She retorted. "The Jamaican woman stuck in the immigration detention centre."

My eyes opened wide. "OMG, yes! That's her name?" I squealed.

Michaela giggled. "Yea, I retweeted your post and a pro bono lawyer is taking over her case." She continued. "We are going to add her issue to the protest and really bid for her to stay as a refugee."

Now I was definitely down to go. "I met her briefly on the day of the fire, but I didn't want to ask her about her business. Do you know her situation?" I inquired breathlessly.

Michaela ran a hand through her ponytail and leaned in for discretion. "She left Jamaica due to domestic violence and she arrived in Canada on a visitor visa. She planned to apply for residence, but she paid a bogus agency to help her handle her application. The ladies who said they would help her scammed her, took all her money, and didn't file her papers. So when the fire broke out that day, she literally lost everything. When she tried to get some help from children's services, they found out she was here illegally. Her children are Canadian, but now she's being deported, so she's fighting to stay here, or else her children will go into foster care. But the good news is, I think we can help."

Those words echoed in my mind. I think we can help. This was the first person at my school to care about this cause, truly.

"So instead of investigating this bogus agency taking advantage of newcomers, they are just deporting her?" I whispered to Michaela.

"Yup . . . so, are you going to come?" she nudged me with her elbow.

"I'm thinking about it. I can DM you and let you know if I decide to go," I said, casually crossing my right leg over the left.

"Yea, let me know for sure," she said.

Francis came back with both hands full of burgers and fries as a server followed closely behind with two big plastic containers of orange juice.

Francis started speaking before I could express my distaste for the "oj". "I know you don't want the orange juice because you only drink water, but they only have Dasani, so I thought "oj" would be a better choice.

"Oh, okay, thanks," I said, standing over Michaela and helping him put the food down on the table.

Good thing I had my full Contigo with me. I thought.

"Hey Francis, this is Michaela, Michaela, this is Francis," I said politely.

"We've met," Michaela said dryly.

"Oh, from where?" he asked, squeezing into his side of the booth.

"I'm a photographer for the Oracle too and I saw you at our first meeting." She said, glaring at him.

"Oh, I see, well nice to meet you again, eh," he said, extending his hand for a shake.

"Nice to meet you," Michaela said, declining the gesture before turning back to me.

"Emily, remember to DM me and let me know. I'll see you around," she said. She stood up and picked up her megaphone.

"What's that all about, is she a source for a news article you're working on?" he asked when she was out of earshot.

"One of my many," I said with a laugh. "I'm surprised you don't know her. There aren't that many people on the team."

He shrugged. "I don't know. I guess her face just isn't memorable," he said nonchalantly.

Changing the subject, I said. "So you're for sure going to the protest then?" I showed him my phone screen with "Francis Porter: Attending" on the list.

"When I RSVP'd it was really just to be polite," he said, shaking a plastic bottle of Heinz ketchup, "but I really think we should go. It would be awesome if I could crack that arson story."

I rolled my eyes.

"What, don't you want to go?" he asked, slathering the ketchup on all his burned fries.

"I didn't say I didn't want to go," I said defensively, picking up a fry and dipping it in vinegar and then my mayo.

"I still don't get that combo," Francis laughed, pointing to the mayo and vinegar.

"That's okay, it's not for you to get," I laughed.

"So why are you not sure about the protest?" he asked again.

"I don't know. It just seems to me that protests have become so performative. It's all for show, now. Remember the last one we went to? Everyone stood there taking selfies and when I shouted 'No Justice' they looked at me like I was speaking in tongues."

Francis laughed. "Yea, that's true. Canadian protests are a lot quieter than what we see on TV from the states, eh?" He laughed before continuing. "But I mean, if Black People Unite is going there, I'm sure people won't be standing around on their phones."

"What makes you think that?" I inquired as I put the last fry in my mouth. I lifted the top bun of the burger and poured the remaining mayo on the American Cheddar before dipping the whole burger into the vinegar. I listened intently to his response.

"*Hellooo*, Black People Unite . . . they are totally aggressive?" He shrugged as he took a bite out of his burger.

"Aggressive or tired of not being heard or taken seriously," I challenged him.

With his mouth filled with food, he waved me off. "Not . . . what I meant." He said in between chewing. "They are about making themselves be heard, so I doubt people will have fun and take selfies the whole time."

"Hmm, right, so are you going?" I asked again.

"Well, yea Em. I'm an Oracle photographer now . . . so yea." He said, grabbing his "oj" and taking a huge gulp, almost finishing the drink in one breath.

I looked down and avoided his eyes.

"Come on, Emily, don't do that. Are you going to be jealous now? Should I not talk to you about newspaper stuff?" he accused.

"What the heck are you talking about? I was the one who brought up the newspaper. Francis shut up," I said bluntly.

"Hey, I was just checking. If you can handle it, then that's great." He said in the usual condescending tone, his hands raised in mock surrender.

"I can handle it," I said pointedly. "In fact, I was talking to my grandmother this morning, and she thinks I should ask Angelique for feedback on my writing. Maybe she can help me improve my skills and tell me why I didn't make it on the team."

"I think it's a waste of time, Em," Francis said between chomping down on his fries and swallowing the rest of his drink. "We're swamped . . . and I doubt Angelique would have the time to give you sound feedback."

I frowned at his negativity. "Yea, because you guys are up to your neck in real journalistic endeavours, right? Tell me again, when does that piece about the lunch lady get published?"

Francis shot me a look and shook his head. "I'm just saying leave it alone, move on sis, focus on something else now."

I dipped another corner of my burger into more vinegar and ate in silence.

"Sound good?" he prompted.

There was an awkward silence for a few minutes as we finished our meals. Francis paid the bill, said bye to a few people, and we left.

"We really should convert to veganism," he said as we waited at the bus stop. "There are so many things we need to cut out of our diet." He placed his left hand on his chiselled abs and rubbed his stomach in circles.

I caught myself staring at his midsection and quickly got a hold of myself. "Yea," I said with an uncomfortable chuckle. I looked away from him and wiped a welled-up tear away from my right eye, "We really should . . . I mean, there are a lot of things we need to cut out."

CHAPTER 11

JUDGEMENT DAY

The rest of the week flew by. On Friday, I breezed through a one-hour English test and handed in two essays. That evening, my dad and I had our weekly movie night. This time we watched "*Troy*". I teased him about how angry he got when Achilles killed Hector. According to him, the disrespectful way in which Hector died made him mad. He yelled at the TV, "How Achilles fi just draw the man pon di grung . . . like him a nuh nuttn? No man, dat rude!"

I took my grandmother's advice and stopped worrying. The entire weekend, I stayed in bed despite my mother's protest and gorged on junk food and fruits. I always added fruits on an eating binge. It made me feel better about the junk food I gorged on. When it was finally Monday, the day of the protest, I woke up excited and anxious. Finally, I was going to talk to Yvette and hopefully, this protest would help her.

It was 10:30am when I woke up to eight missed calls from Francis. *Man, this guy was so annoying sometimes. Obviously, if I were available, I would have answered or called back.* I rolled my eyes and sent him a text.

Yes?

Two minutes later, he replied.

Rise and shine Sleeping Beauty, it's protest day!
I'll pick you up in an hour.

I showered and checked the weather. It was going to be a high of 24 degrees celsius but was currently 13 degrees. That's decent, I thought. I put on black denim jeans, a white v-neck shirt, a taupe cardigan and white ankle socks. I grabbed my black Nike Tanjun sneaker with the rose gold Nike sign and placed them at the foot of my vanity; so I wouldn't forget them. I wasn't a girly girl, but occasionally I enjoyed beating my face. On the days when I felt out of sorts like today, I didn't mind a soft natural beat to complement my simple outfit. I headed over to my full-length mirror after I was done and looked at myself. Sneakers in hand, I spun around again. *My mother will be so proud!* Edges were laid, and I combed my hair in a slick bun. I looked like the daughter she always wanted. With thirty minutes to spare, until Francis arrived, I planned to make a high-protein breakfast. Taking the eggs out of the grey styrofoam carton, I noticed my mother entering the kitchen.

So much for a peaceful Monday morning.

"Morning," I said. "I didn't expect you to be home."

"I bet you didn't. Where are you headed to . . . all dressed up?" she asked.

"I'm going out with Francis," I said.

"Like on a date?" she asked, shocked and stopping in mid-gasp.

"No, he and I are going to a protest downtown."

Just then, my father came down the stairs. Taking the box of egg whites out of my hand and pulling out cheese from the fridge, he said, "scrambled egg whites with Monterey Jack cheese coming right up."

"Aren't you late for work?" I asked him.

"I'm working from home today . . . aren't you going to school?" he teased.

"It's a non-instructional day, no one is going to school." I made a funny face at him and he made one back.

Dad grabbed a red skillet. "By the way, where are you going . . . all dressed up?"

Mom flashed me a look that said, you're definitely not going anywhere now, missy! "Emily is going to a Black People Unite protest." She poured herself a cup of coffee.

"Oh yea it's today, nuh true?" Dad asked as he poured the whipped egg whites into the hot frying pan and topped it with cheese.

"Yea it is, Francis is meeting me in twenty minutes, so hurry with those eggs, pops," I said jokingly, hugging him from behind.

He laughed as he scrambled the eggs and added more scallion. He knew how much I loved scallions. Then a serious expression crossed his face. "You know Emily, mi spirit nuh tek that boy."

I sighed and rolled my eyes. Not this again. "I know, Dad. You say this about Francis all the time."

"And mi a guh say it until you stop talking to him." He said, turning around to pinch my cheeks.

"Emily, for once, listen to your father. I agree, Francis is no good." Mom chimed in.

Suddenly, the doorbell rang, putting a pause on the conversation.

"I'll get it," Dad said, and immediately handed me the spatula before I had the time to rebut. "The eggs are done. Put them on a plate," he ordered as he marched to the front door. My mom bolted closely behind him.

I pulled out a fork from the drawers and started devouring the eggs right out of the frying pan.

"Hello Francis," my father said coldly, opening the door.

"What's up, Frank?" I could hear Francis' cheery voice echo in the foyer as he waltzed into our house with dirty shoes and without invitation.

I walked over to the doorway and greeted Francis with a fork wave.

He was wearing a black and grey oversized hoodie that said, "THE ORACLE" in shiny gold, all capped letters.

As I stuffed my face, he gave me an awkward wave back while his face read: *What are you doing? Let's go!*

My mother didn't say a word to him. She didn't like how kids from Toronto didn't respect their elders. He constantly called my parents by their first name! To them, Francis was entitled, wild and ill-mannered.

Knowing that each of us felt awkward in each other's homes, I scarfed down a few more pieces of the protein meal but didn't finish it. Washing it down with some water, I ran into the foyer. "Uh, hey Francis," I said, approaching the entrance. Our eyes locked on each other. "I'll be ready in a sec, okay?"

He nodded in silence, and I rushed upstairs to brush my teeth again. My grandma always said, "If you eat eggs for breakfast, no one outside of your house should know."

While brushing, I peered my ears toward downstairs to see if I could catch even a little of what was transpiring during my absence.

"So whose idea was it to go to the protest?" I heard my mom ask Francis.

"We both want to go," Francis responded plainly. He always thought my parents were overbearing, overly strict, and he had no intention of changing his usual immature boyish behaviour to make them more comfortable.

I quickly rinsed my mouth, in between the awkward silences at my front door. While drying my face, I kept my hands on my towel and my ears focused toward downstairs.

"Does your mother know you will be at the protest?" Dad probed.

Francis laughed, "She doesn't care what I do, I'm grown."

"Oh, is that so . . ." I heard Mom inquire.

I freshened up and darted downstairs with my black faux leather wristlet attached to my arm. My re-entry pierced through the thick tension in the foyer as Francis stood confidently behind the now closed front door. His arms folded and brows knitted, showing he was getting impatient.

"So what have you guys been talking about?" I asked, playing the clueless card.

"Nothing," Francis said.

My mother was standing parallel to Francis and staring at him out of the corner of her eye. My dad sat on the bottom stair looking straight ahead at him. I stood by his feet and leaned against the dark brown oak railing.

My mother interrupted the awkward silence, "Where exactly is this protest, Emily?" My mom asked me, but she was still staring into Francis' soul.

"Yonge and Dundas square," I said in a jovial tone. I was desperately trying to lighten the mood.

"You need to be back home by 4pm at the latest," she demanded, gracefully shifting her gaze in my direction.

"Well, Marjorie . . . we don't know what time the protest will end, though," Francis interrupted with a laugh.

My mother's hair bounced as she directly glared at Francis again. "Excuse me? It's Mrs. Morrison . . . and was I speaking to you?" she asked. "I am speaking to my daughter."

"Emily," my dad whispered. He was sitting in the Rastafarian meditation position, his large fingers intertwined while the index fingers and thumbs met with their mate. His eyes faced the floor. "Let me give you guys a ride to the subway station."

"That won't be necessary. We already planned to take the bus." Francis interjected. I was still standing next to my father when Francis came over and took my arm. "We should go, or we'll be late, Emily." He said firmly.

My father looked at me with an expression insinuating: *He speaks for you now?*

"Yea, it's cool dad, it's easier to take the transit downtown than driving in that traffic. You know that." I gave a shy laugh again to lighten the mood. Awkwardly, I played with my wristlet. "Bye mommy, bye daddy," I waved as Francis and I walked towards the door.

When we left, Francis accidentally flung the door open so hard that it hit the wall.

"Emily," my father said in a more serious tone, still in Rasta mode.

"Yes . . . Dad," I answered as I turned dramatically.

Slowly, he put his hands firmly on my shoulders. Our eyes made four. "Please be careful. Call me if you need anything."

I scoffed and rolled my eyes playfully. "Okay Dad, I know and I will."

Francis stepped outside, and I gently closed the door behind me to make up for him, almost piercing a hole in our wall.

When we were halfway down the driveway, he commented snarkily, "Why didn't you answer the door? You knew I was coming."

I ignored him.

He shook his head and kept walking.

***

Across the smelly, busy Yorkdale train station, Francis and I walked through crowds. We tapped our green laminated Presto cards on the self-serve payment machine and pushed the loosened metal bar to enter the subway station. Heat from being underground made me sweat, and the smell was usually musty. On the left side of the waiting area was a sign that read "DOWNSVIEW STATION" and "FINCH TO DOWNSVIEW STATION".

I stood in the middle like a divider between both routes, and Francis stood parallel to me. Two minutes later, our train arrived and the automatic doors flew open. The robust, impatient crowd pushed into each other to get in before the doors closed.

Francis and I entered the third section of the train and found two empty seats in a right corner beside the exit door. Without hesitation, we plopped down on the burgundy corduroy-like seats. A few seconds later, the automated voice came over the system saying, "Yorkdale Station, leaving now." The doors instantly shut.

On the fast-moving public transportation, Francis was busy fiddling with his Sony camera like it was a new toy he received for his birthday. Talking about himself incessantly now, he was loud enough that it seemed his words were directed at me but so constant that I couldn't even get a word in. "I'm so excited for today, I hope I get enough photos." He glanced over at me. "Do you think CP24 will be there today?"

I detected a hint of excitement in his voice. *Oh! It's my turn to speak?* I thought before saying, "I don't know. Why do you care?"

He tensed up and sat rigidly in his seat. "What do you mean, why do I care? This could be my big shot, Emily. What the hell? You can't possibly be that dumb, bro."

I was hitting my breaking point with Francis. I laughed in response to his insolence. The type of laugh a black girl did before she popped off. The type of laugh that said, *this bwoy really nuh know mi.*

He looked up at the ad-clattered ceiling with a stupidly wide grin on his face, as if imagining the day he accepted a Pulitzer Prize. "It would be so lit," he said, "if I could crack this arson story."

My right eyebrow raised in disdain. I continued with air quotes saying, "Even if you 'cracked this story', you may not end up on the news today. Today is about the *protest, remember?* So it really doesn't matter if they'll be there or not."

"True," he said cheerily, still grinning at the ceiling, "But if they are there today and I do get them to know my name, they would recognize me when I officially submit my resume to them later." He looked at me with stars in his eyes. "If I play my cards right, I could set myself up and be on my way to working with CNN."

CNN? Since when?

Francis was a star hockey player when we first met. But he broke his ankle last year and spent the entire year healing in physical therapy and writing poetry to cope. Every day I followed him to therapy, and he'd share his poetry with me. I encouraged him to keep going. By summer, he forgot all about hockey and planned to become a poet. Of course, his mother hated this idea and blamed me for influencing him to become an artist instead of a star athlete. But somewhere between August and now, he suddenly became obsessed with being a journalist and it was all he cared about lately.

"I didn't know you wanted to be a journalist for CNN . . . what about your poetry?" I said in a monotonous tone as I played with my phone, not even glancing in his direction.

"What makes you think you know everything about me?" He snapped smugly, completely avoiding the poetry question.

I lifted my head from my phone and glared at him. "I didn't say I knew *everything* about you. But you've literally never mentioned it before September, now it's all you talk about." I countered.

"Whatever, talking about race is all you care about," he replied. His face was serious, and now we were saying hurtful things to each other without breaking eye contact.

The random outbursts of bickering between us were happening more frequently and, as always, there was an awkward silence for a few minutes before Francis continued. "You know Emily, you're an unsupportive friend."

"Well, you're a narcissist," I spat out, unbothered.

"I really can't stand you," he mumbled.

I ignored his attitude. For the rest of the trip, I pretended to be focused on my phone, but really, I was thinking about the last few days. It's like a duppy had taken over Francis' body. He was acting weird, and I had no clue why.

The subway car doors opened to let more passengers in. Luckily it was a station with Wi-Fi. This gave me time to peek at my phone. As I scrolled, a photo of Yvette popped up on my social feed. The headline for the CTV article read: "Black People Unite prepares a protest against woman's deportation." Yvette and her children had been on my mind since our phone call.

Would this protest even be beneficial for them? Maybe I was being pessimistic, but I had a strange, queasy feeling in the pit of my stomach.

Although Toronto was a diverse city, for matters involving Black, Indigenous and newcomers, racism, fear and ignorance always caused needless harm.

I glanced in Francis' direction. He was still playing with his gadget. I scoped him out with intrigue. His hands moved at a fast pace from one end of the camera to the next, and his eyes bulged the way they usually do when he was passionate about something. In deep thought, I looked down, eyes aimed at the floor. Shifting my gaze to a used Tim Horton's coffee cup at the foot of another passenger. It was clear he was hiding something, but what? Why was he so obsessed with himself lately? What type of person was I if I continued to be friends with someone like him? Someone who clearly doesn't regard the feelings of Black people but uses the struggle of my people for his own personal gain. I felt like excommunicating him from my life, but if I did that, I would be completely alone at Trinity. How could I forget, Francis was my only friend? He certainly hadn't forgotten. Maybe he was right. Maybe I wasn't being supportive. If he wanted to be a journalist, then that's a good thing, right? Why should I stomp on his dreams, even if it's unintentional? I glanced over. Francis was aloof.

"I'm sorry for not being more supportive about your dreams," I mumbled.

"It's cool," he said, giving me a playful nudge.

I smiled at him.

He half smiled back. Then turned in his seat to face me. "So, why aren't you more excited about this protest?" he asked.

"Why would I be excited?" I asked, folding my arms across my chest. "It's not some fun carnival type of event," I said, trying to play it cool. "Maybe you don't feel the same way, but I am going for the cause, not for the content." I looked out the window as the subway continued at hyper-speed through the rumbling tunnels. My attempt to be civil back-fired. I knew I struck a nerve with my last retort because, for the rest of the ride, Francis was on his phone, silent, and considering there wasn't any Wi-Fi reception on the subway anymore, I knew he was just trying to distract himself.

After a twenty-minute ride, the train arrived at Dundas station. We exited the noisy, fast-paced underground city and climbed the stairs towards the surface. Tackling a few passersby, we found a spot on the overpopulated escalator leading to the street. Our heads slowly came to the surface of the outdoors and the sun greeted us with a bright and blinding light. There was a rush of people from every corner entering and exiting a variety of retail stores. I stepped off the escalator first, and then Francis followed close behind. We made a sharp left, leading directly to Yonge and Dundas Square. The intersection was filled with people, packed together like sardines and moving in different directions, everyone minding their own business. Suddenly, I felt an instant adrenaline rush mixed with a tinge of anxiety. I needed to find Yvette and her children. *I really hope they show up.*

Francis interrupted my thoughts. "Let's go find where the protestors are." He said impatiently.

"Good idea," I said.

We hastily made our way through the hustle and bustle, me leading the way. I suddenly felt a rush of excitement and determination as we stepped further away from the station. The energy of everyone at Yonge and Dundas square was infectious. People from all walks of life and ages gathered around the four corners of the busy intersection. I looked around for any sign of Michaela or Yvette, but it was hard to see above the crowd. "The energy is crazy here," I shouted in awe.

"Whatever," Francis mumbled, and rolled his eyes. "We should go find some people who are here with Black People Unite."

"Do you know anyone who's coming? Maybe you can text them and see if they are already here."

"Way ahead of you," he said as he pulled his phone out of his pocket and began playing with the screen. Whoever he sent the text to, responded a few seconds later because he quickly said, "Okay, apparently at the next red light, everyone will gather in the middle of the intersection and start protesting."

Just then, all the traffic lights turned red at the four-way intersection and crowds of people flooded the streets at the same time. Astonished by the fruition, I looked back at Francis. "Maybe you really are the next Anderson Cooper," I said, genuinely impressed.

He rolled his eyes and placed his phone in his back jeans pocket. Reaching for his camera equipment, he replied, "It's all about your sources, Em . . . it's called networking, your relationships can get you far." His tone was neutral and his face was stone. It was as if I exhausted him now.

"It was just a joke, Francis," I said, knitting my brows. "What's wrong with us lately?"

"I don't have time for jokes. We didn't come here to joke around right," he said, "We are here so I can cover the story . . . so let's walk faster."

"Listen," I said, interrupting his pace by grabbing his hand. "I don't want to hear about you 'cracking the story' again for the rest of the day . . . I get it. It's important to you. Not the fact that BPU is protesting for what they believe in. I get it Francis, but keep it to yourself. Today, at least, give them the respect of pretending that you are here to be a supportive ally."

I dropped my firm grasp on him and continued walking, then he caught up with me.

"Why do you always have to be so dramatic?" he asked in an annoyed tone. "I'm getting really sick of it."

"Whatever," I said.

"What have you done for anybody, huh? When was the last time you stood up for what you believe in? You talk a mean game, Em, but I haven't seen you lift a finger to make a difference . . . and tweeting about stuff doesn't count." He locked his eyes onto me as he waited for a reply.

I had nothing. He was right. I couldn't even make it on the newspaper team. Clearly, my voice didn't matter to anyone.

A few paces behind him now, I watched him walk further away from me. That actually hurt, I thought to myself.

Francis disappeared into the crowd and before I could even say his name; I lost him. I walked in silence the rest of the way.

Approaching the crowd, I could see groups of people grabbing folding tables and setting up a makeshift conference space in the middle of the intersection. Car horns blared and onlookers pulled out their phones to record. I scoped out the crowd, checking to see if Michaela was around, but I didn't see her. There were several people from Trinity and people from all over the city. I noticed a few Trinity students on the outskirts of the crowd, but other than that, I knew no one else. In the distance, I could see Francis perched on a fancy light post, his legs wrapped around it, as he took photos from above the crowd.

Suddenly, a well known irritating voice punctured my ears. "Hey, Emily!" Katherine said cheerily, with a wave. She was the last person I wanted to see. In an all black Adidas ensemble, her blonde hair stood out even more.

"Hey, I didn't think you'd be interested in something like this, Katherine," I said to her as politely as I could.

"What? Are you kidding?" she yelled erratically. "I am all about philanthropy. See? You should get to know me instead of judging me, Em." She laughed and pulled on an intentionally loose twist out curl hanging in my face.

"Kat..." I said in the same condescending voice as her. "Don't you know you should never touch a black girl's hair?" I gave her a smile that said: *If you touch my hair again, I'm going to stab you with your mascara wand.*

"It's just so bouncy! I love black hair. I wish my hair could go boing, like that!" She replied, continually giggling.

I turned my back to her, looking out for Yvette. *Surely she'd be here, right?*

"So where's your boy, Em?" Her voice made my head turn on a 360 degree swivel.

"My boy?" I laughed. I knew she was referring to Francis, but I had no intention of playing her game.

"Francis, you two are like paper and glue. Wherever he is . . . there you are."

"Hm, that's funny Kat . . . sometimes I think it's the other way around." I smiled and met her bright blue eyes without flinching.

Her cheeks flushed, and she broke our staring contest with a flip of her hair, debuting a brand new hickey on her neck. "Well, I'll leave you to . . . whatever you're doing here, Em. I have an insta-photoshoot in a few minutes and I think I'll save the photos and post it for Black History Month!"

I shook my head, and she walked away into the crowd. As my eyes travelled through the chaos, I saw Yvette. Making my way towards the middle of the intersection, Yvette and a group of people wearing all black assembled a headquarters. As I got closer, I could see a girl with heavy brown hair tied up at the top of her head.

"Michaela!" I screamed over the honking and chanting. Her eyes met mine, and she motioned for me to join her. She bent over and whispered something into Yvette's ears, and she looked up in my direction. At the table where Yvette was sitting was a lady in a taupe pantsuit. She must be the pro bono lawyer. I thought.

"Emily, so happy you came!" Micheala wrapped two arms around my neck, something I didn't expect. Holding my hand, she directed me towards Yvette. "Miss Yvette, meet–"

"I know who she is . . ." Miss Yvette stood up from her chair. Her face was stone.

Great, this lady thinks I probably have a saviour complex and is wondering why I can't leave her alone, I thought to myself.

"Emily!" She embraced both my hands in hers and greeted me with a hug. Since the last time I saw her, she was clean and wearing new clothes. "I was so low the day we met. Thank you for your kindness. This city . . . I always thought everyone was so cold . . . until I met you."

My eyes shot wide open as she continued.

"No one knows how hard it is to come here as an immigrant. No one seems to care. On the day I lost everything, you stopped. You looked at me and you cared."

Now my eyes were filling up with tears.

"It's difficult for me to ask for help in this city. But thank you for showing me that help is available. I've taken the time to ask all these people for help after what you did for me. And now look what happened."

She spread out her arms and motioned towards all the people holding signs and chanting, "No justice, no peace."

Michaela, who was standing behind Yvette, peered over her shoulder to meet my glance.

I smiled back at her. "Okay, what can I do to help?" I said, springing into action.

Yvette took her place back behind the table, so she could get ready for the press conference BPU arranged.

"Honestly, if you could go around and ask protesters to sign this petition, that would be great." The lady in taupe tossed me a clipboard.

"I got it!" I said, turning on my heel and heading towards the left side of the crowd. I could see a bunch of media trucks interviewing protesters near a graffiti wall. If they were being interviewed by the media, that meant they were probably down to sign the petition. I fought my way towards the media trucks when I noticed Francis taking photos of Katherine and two light-skinned girls posing behind her with their fists up in the air.

"Are you effing kidding me?" I said to myself under my breath.

What followed next can only be remembered in moments. I see Francis move a strand of hair from her bright lip gloss. He kneels in front of her and takes a shot. She strikes a power pose and screams, "Black People Unite, fight for your rights!" Her loud voice grabs the attention of Toronto's very own Caroline Cooke, standing near the CTV media truck. Suddenly they are preparing to interview KATHERINE about the Black People Unite protest?!

Katherine!

My legs moved fast, gunning it for the make-shift photo shoot and before Katherine could even get a word out, I grabbed the mic, faced the camera and suddenly I was on live TV.

Say something, Emily, say something. The voices in my head were screaming at me to speak.

When nothing came out, Caroline Cooke prompted."Oh, wow, she's an eager beaver over here. Tell us your name, honey."

I shot her a look and remembered why I pushed down Katherine in the first place. "Yvette Ivy Williams is facing deportation to Jamaica and her supporters, including the Black People Unite Movement, held a demonstration today to protest her deportation." My voice was stern. Strong, the strength my grandma has when she speaks to her clients.

Caroline Cooke's gigantic eyes were fixated on me. Her expression spoke loud and clear: *keep talking.*

I observed my surroundings. On one hand, I could see people were protesting, but on the other, people were standing around on their phones, taking selfies. *I didn't leave my house for this!* It seemed like this was a big show for social media. As if everyone thought: *Let's post that we were here so everyone can see how "woke" we are.*

Suddenly, an unrecognizable force took over my body. Grabbing the sign Katherine posed with, I held it up in the air and started screaming, "NO JUSTICE, NO PEACE, NO JUSTICE, NO PEACE!"

Then Caroline Cooke motioned for her cameraman to follow me. Slowly, people started chanting the phrase with me as I walked through the crowd. I stole an abandoned megaphone from the lady in taupe and begged a tall stranger for a boost. He hoisted me up onto one of the light posts and into the megaphone I yelled rhythmically, "BLACK PEOPLE UNITE! FIGHT FOR YOUR RIGHTS!" Happy that I got everyone's attention, I jumped down from the light post and screamed at the top of my lungs into the megaphone. "This is not a joke! Yvette Ivy Williams is not being heard! They aren't taking this seriously!" I went over to the table with Yvette, Michaela, and her lawyer. They were standing attentively, powerful expressions on their faces.

I continued, "Stop taking selfies and photoshoots and start letting people know how you feel!" I said to the crowd through the megaphone. "How can we expect a change if we aren't taking this seriously?" I walked into the middle of the blocked off street and stood in between the streetcar rails.

"NO JUSTICE!" I yelled.

"NO PEACE!" the crowd chanted back in unison.

Now the entire area was vibrating, and more protesters flooded the streets. More cars honked their horns and more people, on their way to work, shouted at the protestors for holding up traffic.

Still chanting, "No justice," I glanced back and realized that I really built up the momentum here. I riled everyone up! I spotted Francis and Katherine about two rows behind me. Francis had his iPhone lifted in the air, recording the occurrence. There was an intense level of excitement across his face. Katherine was pale and red from panic as she tried to keep up with him. She held onto his back pocket like a child who was afraid to get lost in the crowd.

Like the Pied Piper, I started walking while the media followed. Wherever I went, I led the riled up group of young people onto the streets of Toronto.

"What the hell are you guys doing?" The lawyer grabbed the megaphone from my hands and suddenly the cameras were on her.

She held the black and gold megaphone to her lips, exhaled slowly and then said, "We are here today because Yvette Ivy Williams' life is at stake."

"YEA!" the crowd of followers yelled in unison.

I stood there as adrenaline flowed rapidly through my veins. I was both excited and scared of the repercussions of my actions. *What is going to happen now?*

The lawyer continued. "She deserves to be treated with the same level of respect as anyone else! She needs our help!"

"YEA!" The crowd yelled again.

I curled my fingers in a fist and pointed it at the sky. Everyone got even more riled up. I glimpsed a cameraman from the CP24 in my peripheral. He was pointing the camera in my direction and moving it in a panoramic view. I looked around to see what he was filming.

A fight broke out between a man exiting his car to move the barrier and a protester who was trying to secure the area. In a second, there was a transformation from yelling to fighting as more people joined the brawl. Individuals from both parties began pushing and shoving each other, everyone screaming angrily. This was turning into a riot!

All 5'6 of me was being tossed and pushed from side to side. I had completely lost control. I tried to find Francis but couldn't see him amidst the boisterous, rumbling crowd. He then appeared for a very brief second, standing on the sidewalk and no longer in the brawling crowd. His phone was still high in the air, capturing the chaos. I considered calling out to him for help, but I figured it would be pointless. There's no way he could hear me. It was strange; he was so focused on recording the brawl that his first reaction wasn't to look for me, the way I always looked for him. But why was I even surprised by his actions anymore?

I pushed, tugged and crawled my way over to a cement block, a few metres away from the traffic light, right at the square. I crouched down on the block, in front of a restaurant and watched in horror at everything that was unfolding. It was full-on warfare. Both parties were striking each other with no mercy. Property was being damaged.

A local store manager came out of a convenience store screaming, "What are you guys doing? Who is this helping? Please stop!"

I grabbed my phone out of my pocket. Holding on to it with all my might, I shot a quick text to Francis. It was delivered, but there was no response. I had completely lost sight of him at this point. Next, I took a quick picture of the protest chaos and sent it to my dad. Then I texted:

Can you come get me?

I slid the phone back into safe hiding and kept my hands in my pocket to wait for a vibration.

Then suddenly there was a sea of gunshots. It was ongoing.

I ducked and covered my head with my hands. *I did not leave Jamaica for this.*

"You all have five minutes to clear the area!" A booming voice pierced through the crowd. I looked up for a quick second and realized that it was the Toronto Police. People instantly started scattering in various directions down Yonge and Dundas Street. I couldn't help but think about how ironic it was that protestors were running down two streets with such blatantly racist histories. As I crouched there in a cowering position, I thought about an article I read a few months ago that stated most of the street names in Toronto have an intense racist affiliation. They named Dundas Street after an alleged "founding father" that sought to stop the abolition of slavery, and Yonge Street was allegedly a dumping ground for poor people and immigrants of African, Chinese and Italian descent during the 20th century.

Suddenly, my thoughts were interrupted when I felt an aggressive tug on my cardigan, trying to pull me off my sacred cement block. I started screaming at the top of my lungs. "Let me go!"

"Emily, it's okay, it's just me," the voice said. I turned around and was s o relieved to look down and see Michaela's familiar face.

"Jump down, I have somewhere we can go," she yelled.

Following her instructions, I held her hand and ran with her into the Pickle Barrel restaurant entrance.

"Are you okay?" she asked as we went down an escalator into the basement of the building.

"I've been better," I chuckled.

CHAPTER 12
THE MULTICULTURAL COALITION

I hadn't noticed it outside of school, but Michaela was a kind of badass rebel, without her uniform. In the halls of Trinity, she looked like every other girl, but in reality, she seemed more relaxed.

"You're blessed now, fam," she said, showing off her Toronto drawl with a smirk. I didn't hear this slang accent the first few times I spoke to her at school, but then again, we weren't allowed to use slang at Trinity.

She hopped off the escalator, and I followed suit.

"I feel so responsible for all of this," I whispered as we walked.

"Nah, it's not your fault. I saw everything," she said, giving me a reassuring smile. "It was a stupid Bay street professional trying to break up the protest so he could get to work . . . he started a fight with a protester."

"Yea, I guess, but I definitely feel like I instigated this. I got everyone all riled up."

"Nah, dead that . . . protests are unpredictable. You should know that."

"Where are we going?" I asked, changing the subject.

"Just to meet up with some friends," she replied nonchalantly.

We walked through the underground hallways, known as the PATH, for what seemed like forever. Then Michaela came to a sudden halt in front of a restaurant. She pushed the door open, and the aromatic smell of Chinese food greeted us.

"Why are you meeting up with your friends here?" I asked, confused, as we entered the restaurant.

"With everything going on out there, this is just a safer place," she replied as we kept walking.

So she just has a key to a closed Chinese restaurant? I thought to myself.

We turned a corner, and I saw five people sitting around an expanded circular walnut dining table. They appeared to be in a very intense discussion. The vibe of the restaurant was calm and eerily discrete. It hid in the basement of a major corporate building.

Did they even have customers?

"Emily, these are my friends Aseel, Jason, Jazmyn and Declan."Michaela said as she pointed to each one so I could associate the name with the face. Eight pairs of bright, eager eyes peered up at me in unison.

"Hey," I said, giving one wave to them all.

Jazmyn came over to me and extended her right hand. With my left, I accepted her handshake.

"Hey Emily, it's so great to meet you!" she said excitedly.

"Nice to meet you, too," I said sheepishly.

"Oh, you don't have to say that," she chuckled as her perfectly French manicured hands fondled her type three light brown curls.

"So . . . what am I doing here?" I asked, directing it at anyone.

"It's sort of our little hideout," Michaela said.

"A hideout for what?" I asked. Again, whoever wanted to answer was free to do so. "Do you guys all go to Trinity?" I asked.

"Oh, she asks a lot of questions," Jason said with a sly grin. "She'd fit right in."

Right in where? Where the hell did this girl carry me?

Jason was a tall redhead, about 6'3, with an infectious smile that he sported proudly.

"Do you want something to eat?" Michaela asked.

"Uh, no, I don't. What am I doing here? What are you guys doing here?"

Michaela laughed. "We'll answer all of your questions, Emily, just chill, fam. It's been a long day and we are going to eat. Do you want something?"

"The restaurant isn't even open," I said, as my eyes narrowed in confusion.

A laugh came from behind the bar. "It's my dad's restaurant," a voice said as a 6th person appeared.

"Emily, this is Brayden," Michaela said.

"Hey Emily, I've heard a lot about you," he said with a smile. He hopped over the bar and came to where the rest of us were standing. He held out his hand and I noticed he was wearing a prosthetic arm.

"Nice to meet you, Brayden," I said with a smile.

He winked at me and to everyone else, he said, "My dad is finishing up our orders and then I'll help him take the food out."

"Sounds good," Michaela said.

"Okay then, while we are waiting for your meals, can someone please tell me why Michaela brought me here?" I asked for the last time. If I didn't get an answer, I would leave.

A voice yelled something in Mandarin, and Brayden ran to the back. A few minutes later, he and an older version of him came out with plates of different Chinese cuisine.

"Emily, this is my dad," Brayden said. He greeted me with a smile.

I responded with a "Hi."

After he finished helping his son by placing the meals on the walnut table, he returned to the back of the restaurant.

"Alright, let's eat, I'm marved." Jason said as he reached for the plate of shrimp-fried rice.

Hesitantly, I sat on a chair as everyone dug into their food.

"Okay, Emily, I know you're probably getting impatient now," Michaela said, stabbing her fork in her orange chicken.

"I'm way past impatient, to be honest," I replied matter-of-factly.

"First, no, we don't all go to Trinity," Declan said. "I've known Michaela for basically my entire life. She and I met the rest of the group through mutual friends and family members, and we all just sort of clicked."

"Okay," I said.

"So basically we're a group of friends who are passionate about social justice issues within Canada . . . we're a diverse, multicultural coalition," Michaela said, quoting Martin Luther King Jr.

I stayed quiet, listening intently.

"We run an anonymous blog that, for lack of a better word, attacks all injustices as we learn about them."

"Mhm," I said, mulling over her words.

"We want you to join us. The Activist Coalition is what we call our group," Jason said. "We've been following you for some time. We see your tweets, we know your views, and we love your vibe. We think your sass, blunt demeanour and knowledge are just what we need to take our blog to the next level."

With my hands buried in the pockets of my cardigan, I stared at Michaela, trying to make sense of her and her world. When I finally gathered my thoughts, I said, "I've never heard of the Activist Coalition."

"Well, as Michaela said, we're anonymous," Declan chimed in.

"What Declan means is that," Jazmyn spoke up, "We post very heavy and controversial topics. For our safety, we choose to remain confidential until people can access our blog through a special invite-only."

"Then what's the point of even having a name for your group if no one knows it?" I ask pointedly.

Giggles emerged from all six members.

"A group isn't official until it has a name," Declan responded.

Maybe he thought that by smiling at me, I would like him better . . . but it didn't work.

"Yea exactly . . . plus with our growing audience, we're thinking about finally making our content public and that's where you come in." Michaela continued. "The goal of the Activist Coalition is to report on the injustices of every marginalized community, not just Black people, but Indigenous,

Asians, Arabs . . . everyone. The digital space is growing fast, so it's the perfect way for the information to spread."

There was silence for about three minutes. I guess they were waiting for me to reply to their sales pitch.

"Will you please join us?" Jazmyn asked. "I swear you're my best friend in my head! I'm not a weirdo or anything, but I've always thought you were just one of the coolest people at Trinity."

"You'll have to excuse Jazmyn," Aseel said with an embarrassed, shy smile. "She's just one of your biggest Twitter fans."

"Emily, I'm sorry if this seems like we are bombarding you because that is really not our intention," Jason said. "The Activist Coalition, as you can see, is a multicultural group, and our overall aim is to contribute in our own little way. We are all pure-hearted, pure-spirited people who are striving to achieve equality."

They all sat there with gawking expressions, eyeing me and waiting for my response. It was extremely unsettling. "Listen," I said, my hands still folded comfortably in my cardigan pocket, "I appreciate you guys wanting me in your group, thank you, but this day has been weird enough and frankly this little meeting is icing on a very weird cake." I shifted in my wooden chair and looked at Michaela. "I knew there was something you wanted from me. I really got that vibe from you. No one is ever that friendly unless they have a hidden agenda."

"You really took my approach in the wrong way," Michaela retorted.

I stood and took my phone out of my pocket. With a tight grip on the device, I said, "I don't think so, liking my tweets, approaching me at the bus stop. It was all a part of your plan, that's weird."

"What's weird," Declan jumped in, "Is that you, a girl who professes to be all about Black empowerment, continues to be friends with someone who is not only racist 'as f' but comes from a family that doesn't respect *your* people. How does that make sense?"

I looked at him in horror. "What are you even talking about?" I snapped.

"You can't be that naïve," he said.

"Declan chill," Michaela said.

"No, sis clearly needs to hear this. Francis is racist, Francis' family is racist. Hillel Gardens is a historically racist community. His great-great-grandfather owned house slaves. How do you not know that? And you're his friend?" He asked me rhetorically.

At least I hoped it was rhetorical because I truly didn't have an answer.

"Declan may sound harsh," Jason said, "but he's right. It is really strange that as his friend you wouldn't know that."

I shook my head from side to side. "I have to go," I murmured.

I turned around and fled, dashing out of the restaurant. As I grabbed the handle of the door, Michaela called out at me to stop.

"What is it?" I snapped.

"Yo! Your attitude really stinks, eh," she said calmly.

I rolled my eyes and said, "That's what you stopped me to tell me?"

"No," she said sharply. "I stopped you to tell you, you need to watch out for that Katherine girl too, she's not a friend either."

"Shows how much you know about my life. Katherine is not my friend."

"Whatever," she shrugged. "All I know is last Monday after school, I was heading home and I saw Katherine lurking behind you in the matrix. You should really watch your back with her."

"K, thanks," I said and stormed out of the restaurant.

On the other side of the door, I paced back and forth, my thoughts racing. There was so much to unpack from today's happenings. I really needed to get home. I took the phone out of my pocket; it was 6pm. As expected, there were no text messages from Francis. There were, however, about 50 million calls and texts from my dad that I didn't receive because of the poor reception in the underground restaurant.

I dialed his number instantly.

"Weh the backside, you deh? Look how long mi a call you!" he yelled in my ear.

"Sorry daddy," I mumbled. "I'm fine. Things got crazy, and I lost Francis. Can you pick me up?"

He was silent for a moment. That meant he was livid. "Take the subway to Yorkdale station right now," he said sternly.

"Okay, thank you. See you soon. Love you."

He kissed his teeth and hung up.

I walked towards the subway, returning to what was the abyss of the protest. The stampede of people had disappeared. Traffic flowed at a normal pace. I unzipped a hidden pocket of my cardigan and took out my Aldo oversized cat-eye sunglasses, put them on to hide my tears, and swiftly made my way back to Yorkdale subway station.

On the subway, I was too nervous to sit. So I stood, leaning against a pole. When the train announced it was approaching Yorkdale, I moved directly in front of the door. As it came to a halt, I jumped out and ran to the parking lot to meet my father. There he was, leaning on his car door, arms folded and a perturbed expression on his face. As I got closer to him, he saw my devastated expression and opened his arms to embrace me.

I wrapped myself in his cocoon of love. It was extremely satisfying to have peace after such a chaotic day. Following our embrace, I quickly jumped into the front passenger seat of the car.

The ride home was so quiet I wondered if he had switched bodies with my mother, but that thought was quickly interrupted by the beginning of his scolding. "I knew you shouldn't have gone," he said firmly.

"I know," I whispered.

"Why did Francis leave you? What happened?" he asked.

"What do you mean, what happened?" I asked, confused. I thought for sure he would have seen it on TV by now; I mean, I sent him a picture of the protest.

"Weh you mean, weh mi mean? What happened? How come I am picking you up alone when you left the house with the bwoy?"

I figured that was my confirmation that nothing had been shown on CP24; I was relieved. "The protest got out of hand and was chaotic so I lost Francis along the way," I said.

"That doesn't explain why he left you."

"Daddy, I don't have an explanation. He left, simple," I said, strongly annoyed.

"Oh, so a me you have strength for?" He snapped. "This is the energy you need to be giving the boy, but you have him as your friend and him suh wutlis." A passionate kiss teeth followed his retort.

I sat in silence and allowed my dad to voice his frustrations. He wasn't wrong at all. I kept waiting for an opportunity to defend myself, but everything he was saying was right. Francis was not my friend. Everyone, including strangers, knew it, and yet I still held on to him. As my dad aggressively turned on to our neighbourhood street, I remembered the conversation I had with the Activist Coalition. What they said about Francis' family owning slaves and the history of Hillel Gardens completely took me by surprise. I switched my thoughts from the horrible day to something much better. Like, the warm shower I was going to take later.

My dad parked in the driveway.

As I walked into the house, my mother's angry voice greeted me on the veranda.

"WHAT THE HELL ARE YOU DOING ON CP24 LEADING A RIOT?"

I replied with a knee-jerk sigh. I was really not in the mood for this.

"Marjorie, lower your voice first," my dad said as he closed the front door behind us.

"Don't tell me to lower my voice!" she yelled, but in a much lower tone than before. "Emily, what the hell were you thinking? Why would you put yourself in such a stupid and dangerous situation?"

I kept my gaze on the floor as I made my way over to the foot of the stairs.

My lack of response and remorseful expression did not make her ease up on the berating.

"This has got to be the dumbest thing you've ever done, and you've done some really stupid things! Do you know how embarrassing it's going to be at work tomorrow? My co-workers have already texted me asking if that was you on TV. Did you think about how your actions would affect me and your father?"

"Wait, wait, tek my name out of yuh mouth, Marjorie," Dad said.

"And stop beating up on Emily like this. Did you ever stop to think that maybe she feels bad enough as it is?"

"All you do is pick up for her! No wonder she is the way she is acting like she nuh 'ave no sense pon TV!"

"Can I please go upstairs?" I asked, in exhaustion.

Just then, Mom's cell phone rang. "You try, nuh move. Mi nuh done with you yet," my mom said as she made her way into the TV room to pick up her phone off the couch. She kept going, "If you think mi lef Jamaica fi you come over here, come tun some worthless protestor, you mek a sad mistake."

I shook my head and buried my face in my hands.

Looking at the phone screen in a confused tone, she said to herself, "A who a call mi from a private number?" She clicked the answer button and made a 180 code-switch in tone. "Hello, this is Marjorie," she said in her most polite Canadian voice as she placed the phone to her right ear.

Jamaican parents always do that. Curse you out in patois one second and switch up to a Canadian tone when they get a phone call.

"Marjorie, it's your mother. I just landed at Pearson airport. Someone needs to pick me up, right now."

"I think you put the phone on the speaker by accident," I said to my mom casually, as my grandmother's voice echoed through the house. I knew I was adding fuel to the fire at that point, but I couldn't resist.

CHAPTER 13

MAYBE . . . DEFINITELY

"This is so like you, mother," my mom yelled into the phone. "Why didn't you tell me you were coming?"

I'm not sure what was going on at the other end of the phone at that point because my mother had taken it off the speaker thanks to my big mouth.

"Well, where are you planning on staying?" Mom asked her. "Oh! so you had big plans to stay at *my house* and you just showed up in Toronto unexpectedly?" My mom snapped at her. "Okay, fine, bye." She threw her phone back on the couch and came back into the foyer. "I have to go pick up Miss Patsy." My mother said to my father and me.

Miss Patsy is the name they fondly called my grandmother in her community in Jamaica even though it definitely isn't short for was Anne Marie.

"You two need to clean my house while I'm gone."

"I'm not cleaning anything, Marjorie. The house isn't even messy," my dad said point-blank.

"Listen, Frank, I'm not in the mood to argue with you right now. You know my mother, for her, this house is going to be messy. If I knew she was coming, I would have let the cleaners come yesterday instead of on Friday."

With his car keys in hand, my dad opened the front door and asked, "Which terminal is she at?"

My mom kissed her teeth. "Three," she replied.

"Cool, I'll go pick her up. You stay here and clean your house," he said as he walked out and slammed the door. He hated when my mom referred to the house as hers.

"Emily, I need you to wipe the floors upstairs and change the sheets in the guest room."

"No Mom, Daddy is right. The house is fine. They changed the sheets on Friday when the cleaners came, and it's not like anyone slept in it since." I said.

"Is that backtalk I'm hearing?" Mom asked.

I rolled my eyes and went upstairs. Halfway up the stairs, I called her bluff. "I'm tired and I don't feel like cleaning," I said with my back to her, powerfully marching to my room. I was ready for whatever threats she would make about going for the belt or kicking me out or whatever, but all I heard for the next hour was mumbling about how she had to do everything herself and no one in the house appreciated or respected her. My grandmother hadn't even stepped foot in the house yet and already she had my mother flustered . . . I was here for it.

After washing the horrible day out of my hair and off my body, I returned to my bedroom to put some decent yard clothes on to welcome my grandma. Halfway through putting on my clothes, I suddenly felt overwhelmed. I dropped my grey sweats and plopped down on my bed. Tears welled up, and I started hollering hysterically . . . I couldn't stop. Everything from Francis to my toxic ass parents came flowing out of me. I hated to say it, but even getting rejected by the Oracle attacked me all at once at that moment. I was having a panic attack and started thinking about the punishment I was going to get from my parents. One thing was for sure, they always united in punishing me. I bawled harder as I thought about how mad I was at myself for my outburst on camera. I didn't even want to go to the protest. Why didn't I just follow my gut? Why did I let Francis and Michaela talk me into going when my gut was telling me otherwise? And that weird Activist Coalition crap. What was that about? Remembering that my grandmother would be home any minute, I shifted my thoughts to happier memories in order to calm myself down. I put the grey sweats back in my drawer and removed a black sleeveless cotton maxi dress from my closet. The dress flowed down my silhouette. That's when I heard the garage door open. Suddenly, I ran out of my room and flew down the stairs to meet my grandma.

"Oh, so now you want to come out of your room?" My mom yelled from the kitchen.

I glanced back at her, on my way to open the door that separated the garage from the home interior. My mother was aggressively scrubbing the island with a green scotch brite sponge.

"I'm going to help grandma with her bags, don't you think you should stop cleaning now?" I asked Mom.

She glared at me from the kitchen, and fire emitted from her eyes. "If you think your grandmother is going to save you from being punished, you just wait and see."

I continued on my path to open the door. "Grandma!" I screamed, mostly in shock. I didn't expect her to be so close to the door when I opened it.

"Mi granddaughter!" she said, with her oversized handbag on her arm. "Gimme a hug, nuh!" As I embraced my grandmother, my eyes filled with tears.

As usual, grandma dressed in a classy ivory v-neck cotton blouse with balloon sleeves and black slim pants. She complimented her studious outfit with black suede pumps and a medium-height stiletto heel. She neatly decorated her face with a barely there makeup look, which included a nude lip.

"You cut your hair!" I shrieked, pointing out my grandmother's new hairdo. They cut her natural hair low and had light brown highlights.

"Do you like it?" she asked as she struck a pose.

"I love it!" I said, "So classy!"

"But of course!" she replied with a big grin.

"I've missed you so much," I said to her, my voice cracking. I gave her another big hug.

"Child, I have missed you even more."

We hugged for a very long time until my dad, who was getting impatient standing behind my grandmother, said, "Okay, you two break it up now and move out a di way."

My grandma and I giggled and gave my dad room to pass with the hefty pieces of luggage.

"Are you moving in?" My mother said as she joined us, eyeing the many bags my grandmother carried with her.

"Maybe I am. It's so nice to see you too, Marjorie," my grandma hissed.

"It would have been nicer if you could've been courteous enough to let us know you were coming, ahead of time." My mother hissed back.

"Grandma, get settled in." I interrupted the start of the verbal fiasco.

I gave my mom a look that read: *She just got here, chill.*

In response, my mother rolled her eyes and picked up my grandma's lightest luggage.

"Everyone, grab a bag," my grandma said, "Except you Frank, you grab those two big heavy ones." She pointed to the two large black suitcases my dad dropped by the door when he entered the house.

My dad laughed, "Only if you mek me some oxtail and rice and peas for dinner tonight."

"Oxtail is going to take forever, Daddy," I said. "Can you make some steamed fish and white rice instead?"

"Good point, Em, yea mek the steamed fish tonight and then tomorrow you can mek the oxtail," Dad replied.

My grandmother laughed, "Unnu think mi come here fi serve and slave? Mi come here fi vacation."

The three of us burst into hysterical laughter.

"Okay, well I'm going to go put your bag upstairs." My mother said, interrupting us. She shot us a look before dramatically turning and trudging up the stairs.

***

My mother and I helped my grandma settle in while my dad went to the grocery store to pick up the stuff needed to make dinner.

"So mom, you didn't mention how long you're planning on staying?" My mom said as she unpacked clothes out of the suitcase and put them in empty drawers in the big white dresser in our guest room.

"That's because I don't know how long I'll be staying, Marjorie," Grandma retorted.

As quiet as a church mouse, I took my grandmother's shoes and began placing them in the closet.

"Arite mama," Mom said as she dropped the folded clothes that were meant for the drawers on the bed.

Here it comes. I knew she couldn't hold it in any longer.

"Why are you here? What's up with this spontaneous visit?" Mom demanded.

"You are so fixated on my visit, but do you even know what is going on in your child's life?" Grandma retorted. "I'm here to be of support to my grandchild, something you have never been to her."

I sat in the lotus position with my back facing the women, organizing the shoes in the closet.

"How dare you come into my house with this toxicity! You don't know what has been going on. You don't even live here!"

"Actually," my grandmother replied in a very matter-of-fact tone, "I know exactly what's been going on. I speak to my baby regularly. You're here driving her and Frank crazy as per usual. Everyone is sick and tired of being around you."

"Oh, so you know everything." My mother said, "Well, do you know where your grandchild was today?"

"Yes, she went to a protest."

I crawled deeper into the closet to organize the shoes better.

"And do you know what happened during this protest?" My mother asked. "No? Well, let me show you."

I heard a noise in the background and my voice chanting, "Black people unite. Fight for your rights!" Then it stopped.

In the dark closet, I sighed.

"Okay, so you show me a video of Emily chanting, "Black people unite. Fight for your rights. What's the problem?" Grandma said snarkily.

"Of course you wouldn't see the problem. Frank and I did not raise Emily this way. This makes us look terrible as parents, but you wouldn't see a problem with it now, would you? You actually encourage this type of raucous behaviour." My mom's voice was shaking.

"Raise? Emily a wah . . . chicken?" my grandmother snapped. "She is a young lady with a mind of her own. She has thoughts, opinions and beliefs and how dare you try to silence her voice in a society that already does a good job at that!"

I couldn't take it anymore. "Please stop the arguing," I said in an exhausted voice. "Just stop!"

They both turned and looked at me.

"What is it, sweetie?" My grandmother said softly as she wiped the tears from my cheeks.

My voice was breaking, and I replied, "I can't take the arguing. I can't . . . Why can't we all just get along?" Then I looked directly at my mother and said, "I feel bad about what happened at the protest as it is. I don't need you to add salt to my wounds. I didn't mean for the protest to get out of hand. I was simply standing up for what I believe in. Do you ever stop and think that maybe there is more to life than embarrassing the family? Why would I intentionally embarrass you, Daddy, or even myself?"

"Emily," my mom said sweetly as she approached me gingerly. "The way you acted was completely out of line." She cupped her manicured hands under my chin and said in almost a whisper, "You have been acting like you're an adult these past few days and I have let it slide, but let me just remind you of something. Whether or not your grandmother is here, I am your mother."

She released my face, and I stared at her in disbelief for a few seconds. She continued, "And sweetie? You're grounded for a month. Now go to your room."

After all I said, she still didn't take the time to understand where I was coming from. I looked at my grandmother, who was glaring at my mother with the same astounded expression, but she said nothing. It appeared my mother had finally put her foot down successfully.

I stormed out of the guest room and went to my room. I locked the door and began howling once again. I knew I was probably acting like a toddler with this tantrum, but I didn't care. I felt so lost and alone. After a few minutes, I heard a light knock on my door.

"Emily, it's grandma," she breathed.

"Sniffling and wiping tears, I unlocked the door and went to sit on the edge of my bed."

"Aw baby," she said, "stop crying, come on now, enough of that." She wiped my tears away with the sleeve of her white satin blouse.

"Now listen, I know you are embarrassed about today, but I don't want you to be so hard on yourself. You're young, Emily, and you're going to make mistakes. Look how mi ole and mi still a learn. That's what life is about. Embrace your mistakes and learn from them."

I buried my face in her chest.

"Now let me ask you," she said as she hugged me tightly. "What makes you think that what you did at the protest today was wrong?"

"I don't know," I said.

"No man, tell me. Why do you think you did something wrong today?"

"Because now people at school are going to think I'm even stranger than they thought I was before. Plus, now I am going to have unnecessary attention on me. I don't like that."

"Hmm, so based on what you're saying, it's not that you really think you did anything wrong, you're just worried about what people think?" She asked me, already knowing the answer.

I hate when she does this. "Yes, I guess that's right."

"Emily," she said, pulling me away from her so she could look me in the eye.

"What have I always told you?" she asked.

"Be true to myself," I replied reluctantly.

"Do you think you did the right thing today?" she inquired.

"Yes, but everyone will take this the wrong way," I said.

"I agree with you," she said and pushed a lock of my hair behind my ear. "Let no one, not even me, make you feel bad about something that you believe was right. Stay true to yourself always. Don't just repeat the words, believe them, okay?"

"Okay," I said and gave her a hug.

"Thank you, grandma."

"I love you, sweetie."

"Grandma, just one more thing," I said, as we stopped hugging. "I really don't like it when you and mommy fight."

My grandmother sighed. "I know. I need to work things out with her soon. I've grown tired of the fights myself. She's just so annoying sometimes, man." My grandma said, then we both started laughing like hyenas.

Later that evening, grandma made steamed fish and white rice for dinner. We sat around the fancy dining table, the one we only use for birthdays, Thanksgiving and Christmas, all of us enjoying the feast. Even my mom dove in like she just got released from prison. We all chatted about how happy we were that the weather was still warm in autumn. It was rare by this time of year.

"Man, I want to take a trip to Jamaica soon." My dad said in between bites. My grandmother laughed and shook her head.

"Come, let's fly down together when I head back." We all laughed out loud. Outside of pleasantries and generic conversations, my mother was pretty quiet throughout dinner.

"Emily," she spoke up, "I'll be dropping you off at school tomorrow. I took the day off," She said.

Yep, I liked the quietness better.

"Okay," I mumbled. I decided against fighting her on that.

After dinner, my grandmother and I washed the dishes while my father stayed in the kitchen and kept us company. During the chore, childhood stories of both adults entertained me. These were all stories I'd heard before, but I never got sick of them. I loved hearing about the many mischievous actions my father and his siblings did. Like stealing mangoes off the neighbour's trees. What I enjoyed the most about the conversations between my father and grandmother was that they always ended up with talks of wisdom that made me feel empowered. The lesson I learned today through the childhood anecdotes was to enjoy my youth and not to take life so seriously. My grandmother and my father had such wonderful stories that they laughed about so hard, as if it happened recently. That is because they didn't overthink their lives, they were carefree during their childhood. I went to bed that night feeling proud to be in the family I was in. I was so happy that I was forgetting about the day I had.

***

"Mom, hurry! It's 8:15am!" I yelled from the front door. I tapped my feet as I waited for her to come downstairs and take me to school.

"I'm coming!" she yelled back.

I could have been at school already. I hate when she does this.

"Have a good day at school, sweetie," Grandma said. She came out of the kitchen, cleaning up after breakfast and gave me a kiss on the cheek.

"Thanks, grandma, I'll see you soon," I replied.

My mom came downstairs in a dark-washed denim jacket, a white tank top, black denim jeans and nude wedges. Her face sported a natural make-up beat that was highlighted with a red lip.

"That's why you're running late?" I asked as I pointed up and down at her ensemble.

"Mind your business, Emily," she said. "Let's go, I'm ready." I opened the front door and waved bye to grandma. My dad had already left for work.

The car ride to school was, as it always is, quiet and awkward. I spent the journey journaling notes for a story I wanted to write later.

"What are you writing about?" My mother asked.

"Just thoughts," I said.

"Make sure you come straight home after school," she instructed, changing the subject.

"Yes, I will," I said in a strained tone.

"Don't speak to me in that tone, Emily. I'm still *disappointed* with you," she said, putting emphasis on the word "disappointed".

I remained silent and kept writing.

When she pulled up into the kiss and ride section at the entrance of Trinity, I said "thank you, bye" and hopped out of the car. I opened the left-back passenger door to take out my school bag.

"Emily, I love you. Have a great day," my mother said as she turned her head to face the back of the car.

"I love you too. I'm late so I'm going to the office to sign in." I mumbled and shut the door.

At 8:58 am, I signed in late in the office, took the pink slip from the administrative staff, and made my way to class.

I walked into my homeroom at 9:07am. Mr. Robertson was in the middle of discussing the exam review.

"Good Morning Mr. Robertson," I said. "Sorry for being late." I handed him the pink slip.

"Good Morning Emily, thank you. Take a seat." He took the slip and flung it on his desk.

I made my way to my regular seat in the right corner of the class and sat down as quietly as I could, careful not to disturb the session any more than I already had.

As I sat down, three students in my peripheral area caught my attention. They were sitting in the very last row and were looking at me, whispering. Truth be told, I hadn't noticed them before today, even though we obviously had the same homeroom.

I pretended not to notice them.

"Yea, it was definitely her on CP24 yesterday," the guy whispered. "What a bitch. She's so trash for breaking up the protest like that with her ghetto friends," I heard one girl say.

"They think the world owes them everything," the other girl said.

I kept my head straight and pretended to pay attention to what Mr. Robertson was teaching. Be true to yourself always. I replayed my grandmother's words in my head.

For the rest of the time in class, I took my notes absentmindedly. I continuously replayed my grandma's words in my head, drowning out the stares and whispers that surrounded me. The class ended and the morning assembly was done. Following the virtual announcements, Mr. Robertson told us we were free to go. I waited for the crowd of students to leave and then prepared to leave the class shortly after.

"Hey Emily, please wait for a second," Mr. Robertson said.

"Yes, Mr. Robertson?" I said politely. I figured that this conversation would be about yesterday.

"I gave the final essays back first thing this morning when you weren't here. Here you go," he said as he handed me my eight-page written assignment.

"The rubric is on the last page," he said as he returned to his seat, putting his papers in his briefcase.

I flipped through the pages until I got to the last. *Seventy percent . . .* my essay was on Macbeth, and the topic was to describe the thematic significance of the witches. My thesis was that the witches are the most significant characters in "Macbeth" for three main reasons: they establish the supernatural element that Shakespeare provides throughout the play, the witches present the readers with a clearer understanding of Macbeth's ability to be evil and they are the agents of who bring Macbeth to his own justice. I even presented points of proof for each argument. Frankly, it was a well-written essay, but Mr. Robertson clearly disagreed. After skimming through the rubric, I asked, "Mr. Robertson, may I ask why I got a 70?"

"Your essay was good, but there was not enough information for each argument to prove your thesis. You should have dug a little deeper."

"Oh okay, I understand. However, I was just trying to stay within the page limit you assigned," I responded.

"Some students asked for permission to go over eight pages. If you had more to write, you could have done what they did."

I folded the sheets of paper in my hand. "I didn't know that was an option," I said.

"Well now, you do. So next time, ask your teacher. Don't just rest on your laurels," he retorted.

I stood there frozen at the front of the classroom. *Don't rest on my laurels?* Mr. Robertson stressed to us days after he assigned the essay that if we went over the page limit, marks would be deducted.

"Mr. Robertson, with all due respect, I believe my essay should be reviewed and re-graded. I believe I have presented excellent points for my thesis and convincing arguments. I even have counter-arguments linking other material we have read through the semester," I argued. I was livid, but was trying to keep my attitude in check.

"Miss Morrison, let me be frank. I believe I was pretty generous with my grade. You will still be able to make the honour roll if that is what you're worried about," he said.

"Mr. Robertson I-"

He cut me off with a lift of his right hand. He sighed. "Miss Morrison, go to the principal's office and schedule a meeting with your parents and I, if you want this to be investigated, but I can assure you, the meeting may be to no avail. If your parents are smart, they won't pick up on your behaviour."

"Investigated? That's extreme, don't you think?" I replied.

"I'm sorry, Miss, but I am through discussing this." He said as he took his briefcase off the desk. "Better luck next time," he said. As he walked past me and got to the front door, he turned around and said, "Have a good day . . . by the way, I saw you on the news this weekend." He gave me a look and shook his head. Then he exited the room and left me with my assignment and my thoughts.

I was fighting back hot tears.

Slowly, I trudged through the matrix during the second period spare. Replaying Mr. Robertson's condescending tone in my head, I quickly made my decision. My emotions were telling me this was a clear cut case of discrimination, but was I even right? All the occurrences of the past few weeks left me confused about what was right and what was wrong. Passing the reception office, I glanced through the glass doors. In the upper left corner of the room was a TV mounted on the wall. I watched as the receptionists gathered towards it, stretching their necks to read the same words I was reading: "TROUBLED TEEN SPARKS VIOLENT RIOT".

I felt my ears getting hot when one secretary turned around and met my eyes. She mimed to the others, pointing her chin in my direction. And with that, my fear was confirmed. I thought I was doing the right thing, but now I know everyone else disagreed.

I made my way to my locker, hoping to shrink into nothing with every step. Putting away my binder, I took out my history books to prepare for the third-period class. My plan was to hide in the library until the third period. I entered the school's library behind Trinity in a separate building. When I went straight to the back, I saw the quiet zone.

Perfect, I thought to myself. I could focus on my history notes properly. Following the rules, I took my seat quietly. Opening my history textbook, I began reading.

"Hey," I heard a sharp whisper and felt a tap on my shoulder. It was Angelique. What did the editor of the Oracle want with me? "Hey," I whispered back.

"Can I speak to you outside for a minute?" She asked in a hushed tone.

"Shh," a kid with Steve Urkel glasses hissed at us. He looked like he was in grade nine.

Angelique mouthed "sorry" to him and then looked back at me eagerly for a response.

I nodded and followed her outside.

"So what's up?" I asked in a normal tone once we were out of the quiet zone.

"Have a seat here, please," she said as she pointed to a booth. I slid into one seat, and she sat on the seat facing me.

"I saw you on CP24 yesterday!" she said in an excited whisper.

"Oh," I said as I looked down at my fingers, gently tapping the table.

"No, no, it impressed me!" She said, I guess she caught on to my embarrassment.

"Really?" I replied in astonishment.

"What was so impressive about inciting a violent protest?" Where was she going with this?

"Well, to be honest, when I saw you on TV, it made me see you in a different light. You are exactly the type of person we need to be on the Oracle!" She said and pounded her fist on the table as she said the word Oracle.

I sat up straight and stared at her. "Is that so?"

"Yes!" she said ecstatically! "We need someone as fearless as you to bring that edge to the team. You would be a great fit!"

"Hmm," I said, as my eyes narrowed. I pushed my curls into a fake ponytail with my hands as I mulled over her words.

"So will you join?" she asked eagerly.

"Well, I don't know," I said. "It's sudden. You turned me down the first time. How are you sure you're going to even like what I write about?"

"If you write with the same passion and knowledge I saw on my TV, I am sure I'll love it," she replied.

After a few seconds of thinking, I said, "Okay, I'll join the Oracle, but under one condition."

"Name it."

"I don't want to be limited in what I write," I said sternly. "You are asking me to join the team based on what you saw on TV, right? I want to write about stuff freely, please."

She was silent, obviously pondering my proposal. "Okay, you have a deal," she said.

"Sounds good!"

"Awesome possum," she replied. "We already had our first meeting on Monday but come to the office right after school and I'll give you your first story and the details!"

"Oh, um, I'm actually grounded, so I have to go right home after school," I said in an embarrassed tone.

"Oh," she laughed. "Well, I need you to come to the office and get a tour and stuff."

"I'll make it work," I said. "I'll be there."

"Okay, see you then," she said.

She hastily walked out of the library and I returned to my seat in the quiet zone. I immediately sent my dad a text explaining the situation. He replied:

Don't worry about your mom, I'll handle her. Go to your meeting! Congrats, Boops! So proud of you!"

Even when he's upset with me, I could always count on him. I tried to return to my review, but for the rest of my spare period, I was too excited to concentrate.

When the bell rang, signalling the end of the second period. I gathered my belongings and walked out on air, toward history class. I skipped up the stairs onto the second floor, my heart racing. *Maybe the rest of my time at Trinity wouldn't be that bad after all. Maybe I would actually fit in.* This was honestly the good news I needed to uplift my spirit.

Third and fourth period crawled by. The day took forever to end. At 1:30pm on the dot, I jumped out of my seat and exited my math class. I went to my locker right before going to 4th period to make sure I didn't have to make any additional stops after school. I just wanted to go to the newsroom and then straight home to tell my family the glorious news!

When I arrived at the door that said "Oracle" in big bold metallic letters, I suddenly got very nervous. I opened the door halfway.

Angelique was sitting around a Mac computer with her back facing the door.

I knocked gently.

"Hey, Hey Emily, come in, come in," she said eagerly.

I walked in for the first time.

The room was like a fancy boardroom in a fortune five hundred company. There were four flat-screen TVs hung on the wall. I spotted about six water coolers and in the center of the room was a long black conference table with lots of chairs.

I got goosebumps as I thought about all the stories I would create in this room. *This was a dream come true.*

"Okay," she said as she stood up, "let me give you the tour. First, this is our washroom," she said as she opened a door that led to a mini extension of the already fascinating room. "It's gender-neutral and we keep it spotless. Plus, the cleaners clean it every night," she laughed.

I faked a chuckle.

"Next, these are our water coolers. Our meetings get really intense and we end up talking a lot, so you'll see how necessary the coolers actually are," she said as she giggled again.

I didn't laugh. Instead, I flashed a sincere grin.

"We have our TVs, which we use mainly to watch the news so we can grab the latest scoop."

I cringed as I thought about how my face was blown up on those screens just a few hours before.

"Angelique," I said softly, "Will the rest of the team be alright with me joining?"

"Oh, we already voted! They are all excited to have you on board!" she said.

I released a sigh of relief. "Okay great," I said.

"Don't worry! You'll do great!" She reassured me.

She finished the tour and handed me a contract to review. I sat on one of the fancy conference seats and meticulously perused the details of the contract. It was standard stuff. Confidentiality was important, so I could not discuss the details of the meetings with anyone who wasn't on the team. I had to be prompt for every meeting and wasn't allowed to be absent from over three meetings per semester unless it was a situation out of my control.

"Wow, you'd think I'm working for the New York Times or something." I joked. When I signed my life away to Angelique, she presented me with my first article assignment. The topic was, "Steps we can take, as Canadians, to combat discrimination within Canada."

My eyes danced across the page as I read the resources Angelique provided. "I'm excited," I confessed to her.

"That's great! I can't wait to see what you write," she said!

"Okay, I'll get started right away." I put the paper carefully in a binder and then made my way to the door.

"Hey, can I ask you a question?" I asked her tentatively.

"Sure, what's up?" she said.

"Why wasn't I selected for the team in the first place?"

She sat at the head of the conference table. She hesitated, took a deep breath, and said, "Honestly, Emily, I just expected more from your submission. I was looking for controversial and interesting topics, and what you wrote about was boring. I didn't care about the best Autumn and Winter trends for 2016. Maybe if someone else had written it, but it was below my expectations of you."

I was puzzled, but I let her continue.

"Like Katherine, for instance, she wrote an interesting piece about social media and protesting and whether online advocacy is effective?"

Now my eyes were the size of golf balls while Angelique kept talking.

"It was controversial but still succinct and captivating."

My jaw dropped. "Wow, is it possible for me to read Katherine's submission?" I asked, "just so I can get a sense of what you're looking for?"

"Yeah sure," she said, "let me pull it up."

As Angelique began rummaging through a pile of submissions, I replayed that Monday afternoon in my head. *Did my article fall out of my hand?* No, it didn't because I distinctly remember putting it in my locker. Before I went to the bus stop. Suddenly, I remembered what Michaela said to me yesterday about Katherine following me in the matrix.

"Here it is," Angelique said casually as she handed me the paper.

I read the first line. Then I read the second . . . and the third. It was my article! This bitch stole my article! She handed it in and put her name on my article!

"Thanks," I said calmly as I handed the paper back to Angelique.

"You're right. It's a really excellent paper," I said. It was clear Katherine made some edits.

"Yea it is right? Plus Francis did a little editing for her before she submitted since she was having a hard time meeting the word count."

I blurted out a laugh. It startled Angelique. "Francis is a good friend to Katherine," I said.

"He really is."

"Okay, well, thanks again for allowing me to join the paper. I really should get going."

When I ran out of the room, I thought I heard a faint "bye" from Angelique. But all I could hear was my rapid thumping heart beat and all I could see was red.

CHAPTER 14

LIKE A PHOENIX

This one time, in Jamaica, Ms. Johnson taught us about the story of the Phoenix.

"In Greek mythology, it's known as a mythical bird." She pointed to its picture in our textbook. According to her, it was a magnificent creature that symbolized renewal and rebirth.

She continued, "According to the legend, each Pheonix lived for 500 years, and just before its time is done, it builds a nest and sets itself on fire."

"Cool!" a boy murmured in the desk behind me.

"Not cool, it's suicide!" I blurted out, interrupting Ms. Johnson's teaching. My mouth was wide open and my eyes were as big as Julie mangos. She laughed kindly and walked over to me.

"How could such a beautiful bird destroy itself?" I was confused and looked up at her. She took a slight seat on the corner of my wooden desk.

"Because, Emily, fire doesn't just destroy, it also makes space for something new to emerge."

***

Leaving the newsroom, I barrelled through groups of students chilling in the matrix.

"Look where you 're going!" On my way out of the building, I bumped into Derek yet again. This time, in my rising rage, I was done taking his shit.

"Look 'ere likkle bwoy . . ." I sauntered back towards him, my eyes meeting his, and by his expression, I knew he was looking at the flames in my eyes.

"Talk to me like that again and I'll be at your doorstep with my cutlass." My voice blared out into the echoes of the matrix. I hadn't realized I just screamed at him with all my might.

I felt the stares of students all around me, burning a hole in the back of my head. A few days ago, I would have broken down and called my dad to pick me up, but for the first time within Trinity's walls, I remembered who I was.

"Woo!" I heard a voice call out, and when I turned around to see who it was, I could see Michaela with a group of older students watching the altercation go down. With a pleasing expression on her face, she smiled at me, shooting a thumb up in my direction.

I could hear the whispers and murmurs from all the students watching.

"That's her . . . the one from the news." A football player motioned with his chin.

"She's insane, literally mad all the time . . ." Another girl tried to cover her mouth with her binder as she whispered to her friend.

I took a deep breath in and exhaled, releasing my clenched fists and unclenching my jaw. It wasn't them I was mad at; it was Francis . . . maybe it was just him all along. I was directing all my heat in the wrong direction and at times, even at myself. For not being acceptable or normal. For being an outsider. Maybe it wasn't me that needed to confirm. Maybe I was just in the wrong space. Like a square block trying to fit into a round hole, I needed to find my "fit".

I turned around, facing Derek, who was now leaning up against the wall, hands out, signalling a cease-fire.

I softened.

"Geez Morrison, sorry I was just teasing," He said.

"I get it, Derek, it's just getting a little old . . . sorry I yelled at you," I replied.

The crowd broke up at the sign of no violence, and once again, it was business as usual. I looked at the grand stone walls and the gigantic floor-to-ceiling windows. This wasn't my space, it never was, but before I could even look for a space of my own, I had to tie up some loose ends.

"Ms. Morrison, may I have a word with you?" Principal Kowalski motioned with her index finger, indicating I should follow her to the office.

I guess confronting Francis would have to wait; I thought.

Kowalski's office was like a small cube filled with random things. She placed a photo of her smiley golden retriever on her desk, on the windowsill and on her bookshelf. A stuffed and mounted sea bass hung above her head, and a dog-shaped paperweight lived on top of her mahogany desk. She sat down, facing me, motionless and expressionless. "Before we begin, this is for you." She slid a small white envelope across her wood varnished desk. I caught it before it slid off the table and fell to the floor. I studied the hand-writing on the front.

To Emily, thank you, sweet girl.

From: Yvette

In the envelope was some cash and a photo of Yvette with her children. In all the drama of the past few days, I forgot to pick up Yvette's envelope. I discreetly slipped it into my bag. "Will I need a parent present for this meeting, Ms. Kowalski?" I said, cautiously taking a seat in the guest chair.

"No, no Emily, that's not why I called you in." She said, ruffling through stacks of paper on her desk. She was a tall woman with plain features and broad shoulders.

"If this is about Mr. Robertson or Derek, I just want to say–" She interrupted me before I could continue.

"Ms. Morrison, it has come to my attention that you were on the news over the weekend, at a Black People Unite protest."

I felt my face get hot and my ears started ringing. I opened my mouth to respond, but I couldn't speak.

She continued. "Your outburst led the media to your many tweets about Trinity and some experiences you've had here." She said, while picking up her phone and scrolling through Twitter.

"If only Girl's Day represented all girls at Trinity College *#representationmatters,"* she read, then she looked up at me and placed her phone back on her desk abruptly.

My heart almost beat out of my chest as she continued speaking.

"The Toronto Star even reached out for a comment on some of your accusations about bigotry and prejudice." She got up from her desk and towered over me. Both hands planted firmly on the surface. She leaned in as if she was looking deeply into my soul. "Do you know how embarrassed I felt? Not knowing who you were and how you felt about this establishment?" I could hear a slight quiver in her voice, but her face was still expressionless. She cleared her throat and continued, "At Trinity, we pride ourselves on excellence . . . and how we've made you feel here, is not excellence."

She took a deep breath in before walking over to me and taking a seat in the second guest chair in front of her desk. "Emily, it's not your job to teach us how to make you and others feel more comfortable at Trinity College, we've clearly dropped the ball on that, but I'd truly like to know more about your experiences here, so I can at least use your feedback to make some changes around here."

I exhaled, not realizing I was holding my breath and expecting a blow to the chest in the form of an expulsion. Almost letting a tear out, I said, "Where do I even start?"

She placed her hand on mine as it rested on the arm of the chair.

"Start from the beginning, Emily." Ms. Kowalski answered.

***

When I arrived at the bus stop, I caught the transit just before it left.

Perfect. Sitting on the seat right behind the driver, I replayed the events of the day in my head. Was I in the twilight zone?

Ding A notification popped up on my phone, and it was a message from Francis. Impatiently tapping my feet on the floor, I waited as the photo message downloaded. The text read:

Sorry Em; I know you tried your best, but you can't save everyone.

When the photo finally loaded, I understood the context of his message. "A Jamaican Immigrant Woman Fighting to stay in Canada gets deported." I felt heat in my chest while hot tears burned down the sides of my cheeks. With every stop the bus made, I got more agitated each time. I wasn't done with the fire that was brewing inside. There was more "clearing" to do.

Finally, my stop appeared. I stood up and held onto the red post, pressing the red button. When the bus driver came to a halt, I jumped out, thanked him and began walking on a mission to Francis' house. With each step, I thought about how I was going to approach Francis. This was too unique a situation, so I had to be stealthy about it.

Hey, I need a pick me up, I'm coming over . . .

I texted him while walking to his door. He clearly had his phone in his hand because he replied right away.

Hey, stranger.

Hey stranger? Okay, calm down. I reminded myself.
Can I come over?

I'm shooting for the paper, let's take a raincheck.

But your room light is on.

I could see his light from the end of the long suburban street. The three grey dots appeared and disappeared about five times within a minute before he sent his next message.

"I'm shooting inside, now's not a good time."

"I'm almost at your house though,"

Again, the dots appeared and disappeared.

Can I call you later?

Sure.

I flung my backpack around the front of my body and put the phone in the small part of my bag as I walked up to his driveway.

Arriving at the door, my fingers glided over the silver keypad lock. Since the first day I met Francis, he shielded his home passcode from me like I was some kind of criminal. Now, it would finally come to good use. I input the numbers "0212" and his front door unlocked with little of a sound. The code was his mother's birthday, February 12th. I entered the house stealthily and closed the door behind me. I knew how particular Mrs. Porter was about her hardwood floors, so I took my shoes off quietly and kneeled down to place them beside my schoolbag, which was now in a corner by the closet.

"What the hell?" Francis asked, standing at the top of his stairs.

I stood up and looked up at him.

"What are you doing here?" He asked, running down the stairs.

Without a word, I walked past him and up the stairs towards his room.

"Are you dumb? I'm talking to you," he yelled, grabbing my left wrist. Now he was below me, tugging me.

I looked down at him and calmly said, "Let me go." It was a firm but quiet tone.

In his shock, he did as he was told.

I continued up the steps.

"Emily, what the hell is wrong with you? Just wait a second!" he barked.

I stood at his bedroom door entrance and pushed the half-opened door.

There she was, sitting on the bed with her legs crossed, typing aggressively on Francis' MacBook Pro. She looked up at me, unconcerned, and continued with the laptop.

Now he was standing at the top of the staircase, which was some distance away from his room door. He knew better than to come any closer to me now.

I turned around, tilted my head to the side, raised my eyebrows, and gave him a knowing smile.

"What the fuck are you doing walking into my house like you own the place?" he asked.

"Oh, so we're flipping the script?" I asked. "Before you act as if you are actually angry about me showing up here, let me just warn you I know you better than you know yourself."

I walked up to him and jabbed my index finger in the right side of his head. "Tell me how Katherine got my bomboclaat article!" I yelled.

Francis and I had known each other for long enough that he knew when the Jamaican bad words surfaced, It meant trouble. His face got beet red as he nervously rubbed the back of his head and looked down at his feet.

"What are you talking about, Emily?" he asked, his voice quivering.

"Francis, do not let me set this bloodclaat house on fire with all three of us in it," I said in a matter-of-fact tone.

"She's threatening y–!" Katherine yelled as her apple-shaped head peeked out of the room.

In a second, I lunged at her, and Francis grabbed me by the waist.

"Francis, get her away from me!" she yelled, "This bitch is crazy!"

"Is everything okay up there?" Mrs. Porter's voice appeared as I heard the front door close.

"Yes mom, everything is fine!" he yelled back.

"Francis, let me go!" I screamed, turning to face him.

"Are you sure, Francis?" His mom asked. I could hear a glass of wine in her voice.

"Mom, everything is fine, please just leave us alone!"

"Let's go in the room," he mouthed to me.

I ran into the room and watched Katherine standing nervously in a corner by the closet.

"Listen, I'm not leaving until you tell me two things. How and why?" I began after he gently closed the room door and we were all trapped inside.

"How did Katherine get my article and why did you help her edit and submit it if you 'thought' it wasn't a good piece?" My index and middle fingers curled over my head as I used air quotes. "Stay there," I commanded Katherine. I could hear her attempting to move over to the bedroom door where Francis and I were standing. "Francis. Tell me everything," I said. My voice was shaking from anger.

"Can you sit down?" He said nervously.

I leaned against his door frame and folded my arms. "Start fucking talking," I said.

He plopped down on the bed. "I've never heard you swear this much. It's making me uncomfortable," he said, rubbing his neck again.

"Francis, I am not the one–"

"Okay, okay, okay," he said in a strained tone. He moved his hands up and down as he spoke. "You know . . . the Caldwells all end up at Ivy League schools, right . . . ?" His hands were shaking as he spoke.

"Francis, if I have to sit here and listen to a speech about the plight of being rich, white, entitled, and privileged while getting into Ivy League Schools, I'm going to go mad." I interrupted him, "Please get to the point!"

Francis looked at Katherine, then back at me, and continued with a deep sigh. "My mom told me to have dinner at the Caldwell's the night I ditched you at the bus stop. That's why I was in a rush."

I nodded, urging him to keep talking.

"The student advisor her parents paid to get her siblings into Harvard, was there, and he started talking to us about our futures. How it's important to get into the right schools, with the right degree, which careers make the most money . . ." His voice trailed off. He looked as if he was about

to cry. When our eyes met, he looked down at the floor and cleared his voice. "Anyway, she needed to get on the newspaper team to add more extracurriculars to her student resume. I knew I could get her in, she just needed a story."

Now my eyes were filling with water, but I wouldn't let them go. I wouldn't give them the satisfaction of seeing me cry. With my eyes fixed on Francis, I said, "Say no more."

"I'm sorry, Em, I told Katherine about your paper because I knew you weren't confident enough to submit it," Francis mumbled to the floor.

"I was confident about it. You broke that," I uttered as a tear rolled down my cheek and I quickly brushed it away. "I trusted you . . ."

Francis looked up at me. His face was blotchy and red, and his eyes were filled with tears.

"So then I-" Katherine started saying, but I put my palm up to tell her to stop.

"If you knew what I knew, you would not send your words in my direction," I said, arms folded around my body. I held myself because I couldn't look at her yet. "Francis, continue," I said to him.

He sighed, "Katherine, I'll tell it," he said, looking at her with a pitiful look, saying I'm sorry.

I cleared my throat and looked at my feet, then looked back up at him.

"Alright, so on Monday when you saw Katherine at the Oracle's office, she followed you to your locker and waited until you left. Everyone knows your locker's been broken all year, so I told her how to open it."

I uttered a small, quiet chuckle as he continued confessing.

"She made a copy of your story and put the original back, and I edited the text enough to make it seem different. Then I emailed it to Angelique."

I wiped my face with my hands and looked over at Katherine, who was still standing by the closet, her hands by her side like she was training for cadets. "So I got the how. My next question is why? I thought we were friends," I said to him.

"We are friends," he said, "But . . ."

My brows knitted, waiting for an answer.

His head hung so low, his shoulders hunched over. I couldn't see his eyes, but I could see a few solo tears falling from his face and onto the carpet.

"Listen Em, this is more than high school games," Katherine said, building up some courage. She gracefully walked over to him, "My student advisor says couples who stay focused on their goals together have an 89% higher chance of getting into the same Ivy League School." She took his right hand and intertwined her fingers with his.

"Wow . . . congrats," I said, still keeping my gaze on him. I took a deep breath, clasped my hands in front of my face and turned to walk out of the room when suddenly I turned back around. "You know, your mom told me about your dad," I said. "She was drunk and told me everything. She was an embarrassment that day." I hoped my words hurt him.

"So you have secrets too then," he said, standing up.

"What was I to you?" I asked, ignoring his feeble response. "Just a charity friend? An experiment so you could understand why your dad left you and your mom for a black woman?"

"Are you fucking kidding me, Em!" He yelled, placing both hands on his hips. "Do you know who my family is? How I have to make up for my father's mistakes?" His face was violently red. "I'm a Porter! There are buildings named after my grandfather! I don't have the luxury of just being a poet or even liking whoever I want to!"

His voice was like thunder now.

"You may live in Hillel Gardens, Emily, but until you understand how this all works, you shouldn't judge what you don't know." Katherine said, grabbing her bag, "Good families date, into good families." She flipped her hair to the side and reached for her jacket. "Okay Francis, just text me later when you've solved all of this. I have to go," she said sweetly and planted a wet, disgusting kiss on his lips.

My eyes locked with her as she exited the room, but when she got to the door, I grabbed her wrist. "No, you stay. I'll leave. Go sit down and forget about trying to make a dramatic exit." She looked at me in disbelief.

I rolled my neck and glared right back at her. Francis held his face in his hands now, and she went to sit with him.

I turned around and made my way down the stairs slowly. When I started putting on my shoes at the closet door, Mrs. Porter hollered from the kitchen, "Hey Emily, next time please put your stuff inside the closet . . . with the blacks."

Of course, this woman would pretend as if she didn't show me her ass the other day. I thought to myself. "I'll be sure to do that, Mrs. Porter," I said. I turned the knob and walked out of the house.

CHAPTER 15

COME WITH THE FIRE

The next day, I rolled over in my bed and released a heavy sigh. For a moment, I felt the urge to grab my phone and text Francis, but quickly remembered that last night's nightmare was real. It's funny how change feels. One day you know someone and the next, you wish they never existed. In mid-stretch, my phone vibrated, and I reached over to my nightstand to pick it up.

"Hey girl, are you okay?"

Michela asked. She witnessed my outburst with Derek and was actually being a good friend and checking in with me.

Yea, I'm fine

Truth is, I wasn't sure what I was. Last night I fell asleep somewhere between the first "Why did I marry you?" and the last "Guys, stop the fighting!" My parents were still out of control, even with my grandma here. I slowly got out of bed and made my way downstairs.

My dad was sitting in the TV room watching the news absentmindedly.

I came to a halt at the entrance of the TV room and leaned against the wall.

He noticed I was there after a few minutes. "Hey Boops," he said. "Come sit beside me."

"You're not mad about the protest anymore?" I asked, almost afraid to hear the answer.

"I'm still disappointed in you," he said, putting emphasis on the word "disappointed," but you a mi one pickney a d end of d day. He gave me a hug, and I melted into his arms. I really needed that hug from my daddy.

"So what are you going to do today?" he asked me.

"Study, I guess. Maybe do some writing," I said. I winced. I probably shouldn't have said the word' writing. "What are you going to do?" I asked him.

He sighed. "Hey, do you want to watch a movie?"

"Now?" I asked.

"A wah? You have school fi guh?" He teased me.

I laughed. "Okay, let me get some cereal," I said as I jumped off the couch. "You choose the movie and I'll meet you down there."

As I made my way to the kitchen, I asked him, "where's grandma?"

"You know the ole woman needs her morning walks. She should be back soon," he said as he walked down the stairs and into the basement.

I quickly poured some Nesquik and unsweetened Almond milk into a bowl, grabbed a spoon, and started for the basement.

In the basement, I sat down on the couch and wrapped my right leg under my left while diving into my cereal.

My dad placed his coffee mug on the wooden table and said, "I'm in the mood for a Madea film, weh you seh?"

"I'm always in the mood for a Madea film," I laughed.

We decided on Madea's Family Reunion. We got to the scene where it was the family reunion and the mother (the legendary Lynn Whitfield) and daughter (Lisa Arrindell Anderson) were fighting. My dad paused the movie.

"Emily," he said in a soothing voice, as he turned his body around to face me. "Your mother and I are getting a divorce."

My cereal had finished a long time ago, but I still had the bowl and spoon in my hand. I placed it gently on the table.

"Hmm," was all I could say.

"How do you feel?" He asked as he placed his hand on my knee gently.

"Does it matter?" I asked, looking up at him.

"Of course it matters. Come on man, talk to me," he said.

"I don't know how I feel, to be honest. I guess I should have seen it coming."

"Come here," he said, and I buried my head in his chest.

"This is for the best. Your mother and I have come to an understanding. We will always care about each other, but we are not fit to be partners. You understand that, right?"

"Yes, I do," I said.

"There's one more thing," he said, and I felt his chest move dramatically as he inhaled and exhaled. "I'm moving back home," he breathed.

I pulled out of his arms. "What? Daddy–" Then I stopped. For once, Emily, don't think about yourself. "I understand," I said with a sigh.

"I'm not happy here, honey. And I have only held on this long because of you. But you know you can visit me or move back if you want. I'll always be here for you," he said.

He kissed my forehead.

"I know daddy."

"Are you happy?" I asked him.

"Yes, I am happy. I'll be happier if you are happy," he said.

I laughed. "I am happy if you are happy," I replied. "I just don't know how I'm going to live with mommy all by myself," I half-joked.

He chuckled. "It may work out better than you think," he said. "I'm the one that made her miserable, not you."

"I love you, daddy," I said to him and gave him another hug.

"I love you too Boops, I love you too."

I watched the rest of the film cuddled in his arms.

When the movie was done, daddy and I made our way upstairs.

He left for the gym and I could see my grandma was back from her walk and prepping to cook.

"What are you cooking?" I asked her.

"Chicken foot soup," she said.

"Yes!" I said, laughing. "Want some help?" I asked.

"Yes man, come knead the flour."

"No, mi cannot do that," I giggled.

"I know, I just wanted to hear you say it," she teased and playfully slapped me on the buttocks. "You know your specialty already, chop up the seasoning."

I grabbed a cutting board and took the scallion, thyme, onion, scotch bonnet peppers and garlic out of the fridge.

Chopping up the scallion, I said, "they're getting divorced."

"I know," she replied plainly. She was cleaning the chicken feet. "How are you handling that?" She asked.

"It took me aback at first, but I know it's for the best. If they'll be happier apart, then I'm all for it."

"That's a very mature attitude," she said, giving me a quick kiss on the cheek.

"I cyaan hug you. Mi hand raw from the chicken," she laughed.

I laughed with her.

"Well now, you have two very excellent reasons to visit more frequently," she said as she drained the vinegar water from the chicken and added fresh water and vinegar.

"Daddy said I can move back if I want to."

"I don't think you should, at least not right now," she said.

"Stay here, finish school, go to university or college, whatever, then move back if you still want to."

"That's a good point," I said with a nod.

I pushed the chopped scallions to the top of the board and then started on the garlic and onions.

"How's mommy doing?" I asked her.

"Oh, you know you madda, who knows how she's doing?"

"Do you think she'll talk to me about it or she'll just pretend like it's not even happening?" I asked.

"Let's wait and see, you never know," my grandma replied. "Mi need some music inna dis place. Put mi Beres Hammond CD inna the radio deh."

"CD grandma? Inna big, big 2016? We've talked about this," I teased.

I ran upstairs and grabbed my Bluetooth speakers. I found her favourite track, "Tempted to Touch " and let Beres' smooth voice caress the kitchen. Grandma inadvertently started moving her hips and shoulders to the mellow beat, then she started sing-ing the lyrics. "Good vintage whine sweet conversation you and I, Let's start it." She sang out.

I danced along with her and started singing the lyrics. We danced along to each Beres song that played until she requested Freddy McGregor. We danced and sang together until dinner was all done and the kitchen was spick and span.

Later on, when my mom came home, we all had dinner together in the kitchen. It was surprisingly not as awkward as I thought it would have been. The conversation was polite and generic, but at least there was no bickering. After dinner, my mom offered to do the dishes. My grandma and my dad settled in the TV room for the rest of the night, watching the various news channels.

Still feeling drained, I made my way upstairs to wash up and change into a white plain oversized t-shirt and black cotton shorts. I was sitting around my desk, oiling and massaging my scalp, when I heard a gentle knock on the door.

"Come in."

"Hi darling."

"Hey mom."

"Do you need help with that?"

I hesitated for a second and then I said softly, "sure."

She took the DIY bottle of castor, avocado, and grapeseed oils from me and sat on the edge of the bed. Placing it on the floor between her legs, she said, "sit here."

I sat in between her legs and she oiled my scalp.

I forgot how much better a scalp massage felt when another person did it.

"So daddy said he spoke to you about something?" she said.

"Yes, he said you guys are getting a divorce," I said pointedly.

"How are you doing with that?" She asked.

God, please let this be the last time I hear this question. "I'm okay now," I said. "It's for the best."

"Yes. It is for the best," she said. "Turn to the right," she instructed. I turned and my mother started oiling the right side of my head.

"Emily, while I am still very disappointed in you for what you did, I am more hurt that I had to find out from your principal how much you have been hurting," she whispered.

"Turn to the left," she said when she was finished with the right side.

Turning, I said, "She called you? I don't really know how to speak to you about things."

"I realize that, and I really want us to work on that. So I have an idea. Would you come to therapy with me?"

"Therapy?"

"Yes," she said as she began finger detangling my hair. "Where's your leave in conditioner?"

"In the bathroom."

"Okay, can you go get it, please?" she asked. "I'll just twist out your hair."

"Okay,"

As I made my way to the bathroom, I wondered if this was some sort of trick. Therapy? As in, to fix the issues between us? Why now? I picked up my leave in the conditioner and spray bottle and returned to the room. Sitting in between my mother's legs again, I asked, "Mom, where did this therapy idea come from?"

"To be honest, Em," she said. "I have been toying with the thought for a while that you and I need to reconnect, but I just didn't know how to approach you. It was actually your grandma who suggested that we try."

"Wow, Grandma did?" I asked in shock.

"Yes, she did. Last night she and I had a long heart to heart after I spoke with your dad. It was a very long night," she laughed.

"And your grandma and I addressed things we needed to address for many years now."

"That's fantastic," I said, and I meant it.

"I miss the days when you would come to me and talk to me about anything."

"That was a long time ago," I said with an awkward chuckle.

"I know," she said. "I want to understand you. I want you to understand me, especially now since it will be just the both of us primarily."

"At least I hope," she said after a few minutes.

I stopped to ponder for a second. *Where was my home? Was it Canada or Jamaica?* I closed my eyes to decide for myself. "Yes, it will just be the two of us here," I responded. "But I really need to change schools, mom."

She kissed the crown of my head. "Okay love, we're going to make a lot of changes."

After a few minutes, she held my head in between her hands and said, "All done."

"Thanks," I said.

"You're welcome."

"You can put the leave-in and stuff on my desk."

"No, it's fine. I'll put them back in your bathroom. You know I don't like when things are out of place," she said firmly.

I laughed, "Yes, you're right."

As I wrapped my hair with my satin head tie and got cozy in bed, I thought about one thing. I guess Francis and Katherine weren't the only two with "good" families.

The next day, after homeroom, I journeyed through the matrix to revisit my old rusty friend, the locker. While I was exchanging first period books for third, Michaela came up to me.

"Hey girl, hey," she said. "How was your weekend?"

I laughed, "Not bad at all, girl."

"Hey so," she said, leaning on the locker beside me. "Have you thought any more about joining the Activist Coalition?"

"Actually, I have, after finding out the Canadian Border Services deported Yvette last week, I feel like it's my duty to help now." I said.

"Really?" she asked, genuine shock exuding her mouth.

"Yea, I have thought about it." I said, as I slammed the locker closed. "I'm quitting the Oracle today and changing schools in a few weeks, so I'm down to join . . . but I really think you guys should stop posting anonymously," I said.

Michaela laughed and nodded her head in agreement as we moved down the matrix.

"Where are you going? Do you have class right now?" I asked.

"Nah, I have a free period. I was actually going to meet up with the coalition."

"I have a free period too," I said. "Can I tag along?"

"Sure!" she exclaimed.

As we walked to meet her friends on the benches outside, I heard my name over the loudspeaker. "Will Emily Morrison please come to the main office?"

I lifted my head and dropped my hands on my binder.

Michaela laughed. "We have a rebel in our midst," she said with a wink.

I shook my head and said, "I'll see you later if I'm not back by the time the period ends."

When I entered the main office, I approached the secretary with the wild auburn hair. "Hi, I just heard an announcement over the PA system asking me to come to the office," I said. "My name is Emily Morrison."

The secretary laughed. "Oh, we definitely know who you are, you're our little celebrity. Please have a seat," she said.

I shrugged my shoulders and sat in the chair right beside the principal's office. I wasn't even nervous because I knew I did nothing wrong, but I was annoyed. My name was too easy for these people to call. Ms. Kowalski came out of her office. "Miss Morrison, welcome," she said, with a bright smile that actually looked genuine. "Do come in."

I followed her, and another lady stood up upon my entering. She was about 5'8, blonde and wearing a cute fit and flare knee length floral dress with no straps. She accessorized the fashionable outfit with an adorable mint green tote bag and nude pumps. "Hi Emily, it's a pleasure to meet you," the well-dressed lady said as she extended her hand for me to shake.

"It's a pleasure to meet you too," I said, with a confused look.

"Oh, sorry, how rude of me," Ms. Kowalski said.

"Emily, this is Kathleen Goldberg. She is a Regional Human Resources Manager at the Toronto Spectator."

I nodded. "Nice to meet you, again," I laughed.

"Please have a seat," she said, pointing to the seat beside her.

"Would you like to do the honours?" the principal said to Kathleen.

"Sure," she said excitedly. "Emily, I'll cut to the chase. The Toronto Spectator team would like to offer you a part-time position as a student journalist writing an opinion column," she revealed with a massive grin on her face. Her nude glossy lips shimmered against the sun that peered into the office.

"What?" I asked, looking from her to Ms. Kowalski.

"Angelique James shared an article submission you wrote for the

Oracle . . . we were very impressed with your knowledge on social justice issues," she said. "While we believe you need to learn just how to express your opinions, we think you have interesting opinions that need to be shared with the world. This position will enable you to strengthen your writing and editing skills!" she said with the same level of excitement in her voice.

"Wow, um, I don't know what to say." I was stunned. "This is so unexpected."

I felt my phone vibrate, but this was no time to check it. "Wow," I said again. "Sorry, I'm not saying much, I know." I laughed nervously. "But yes, I'd love to be a part of your team. What is the salary commensurate with the position?"

She let out an impressed laugh. "I like you, Emily. No beating around the bush. The salary for this position starts at $18 hourly, however there is a strong possibility of a pay increase and bonus opportunities," she said.

"Hmm," I said, nodding. "Okay, not bad."

"I will email you a detailed offer letter and contract, so don't worry, this is not just a verbal offer," she said.

"Sounds excellent!" I said. "Thank you very much."

She nodded, "You're welcome."

I sat there for a few seconds and then I said, "Is there anything else?" I really meant it politely.

She laughed, "Nothing else, Emily. I will send the details to you. Is your school email okay?" she asked.

"Actually, I prefer my business email. May I take a sticky note?" I asked the principal.

"Yes, of course," she said.

I borrowed the pen and wrote my email address on the sticky. Then I handed the paper to her.

"Excellent," she said. "I will send it to you by the end of the day."

I stood up. "Thank you so much. I look forward to working with you." I extended my hand for a final shake.

"Have a good day, Emily," she said with a smile.

"You as well." My heart was beating out of my chest as I walked out of the main office, but I kept my cool.

The last bell rang as I entered the matrix. I was so excited about this job. For once, everything seemed to be falling into place, but I had one more job to do. Today I planned on telling Angelique I was quitting the Oracle.

When I got to the Oracle office, I pushed open the door, and I found Francis and Katherine sitting at the boardroom table. Her face was in her hands as Francis consoled her. Before I entered, I armed myself with a deep inhale. With blinders on, I hurried into the room, gunning it for Angelique's desk.

I'll grab a piece of paper from her desk and leave her a quick note to call me. I said to myself internally.

"What the fuck are you doing here?" I heard Katherine's voice blurt out. I continued writing my note, ignoring her in the process.

When I was done, I placed the note on Angelique's agenda and started walking towards the exit.

Katherine sprung up from the table and extended both arms in front of her, blocking my way out of the room. "Oh, you're not going anywhere." Now she was blocking the door with her body, leaning on it and then locking it from the inside. I looked over at Francis, his eyes were pointed to the floor. He looked like he hadn't slept; he wasn't looking my way.

"You know, Emily, I knew you were a loser, but I didn't realize you were a rat as well." She said, staring straight at me. For once, Katherine looked dishevelled. Her eyes were red and puffy from crying, and her hair was in a messy bun on top of her head. I remained calm as she continued.

"I can't believe you told Principal Kowalski I plagiarized my submission piece. Not only am I kicked off the Oracle, but now I have no chance in grabbing the student journalist position at the Toronto Spectator." She said, between tears and screaming. I reached for the doorknob and she moved to the left, blocking it with her back.

"Katherine, I don't have time for this seriously and I didn't tell anyone." I said, exhausted by her victimhood. "Francis, please remove her from this door before something bad happens." I warned in a monotone voice.

Her eyes grew larger and in her emotional state, she began panting, rage rising with every breath.

"What are you going to do about it, Emily?" Her hands were clenched into fists.

In an instant, I stepped closer to her, studying the anger on her face and her smug expression. I would not let this get to me. In a few weeks, I'd be out of Trinity and at a new school with new opportunities and friends; I would not mess this up. "I'd like for you to move out of my way, please." I retorted.

Now Francis was watching from where he was sitting.

"Francis, move her now!" I shot a look at him. He got up slowly, making his way towards both of us.

"Katherine, just move aside, I don't want to deal with this right now." He sounded exhausted.

"How can you defend this bitch!" Katherine's words were like venom. I hadn't ever seen her like this before. Her usual perfectly preppy exterior had faded, and now I was looking at a woman having an existential crisis.

"Katherine, if you lost anything, it was because of your own toxic actions, not me. It's not my fault they chose me for the student journalist position at the Spectator . . . I earned it."

From her expression, I realized I had just made things worse.

She let out a hysterical laugh. "You!" She was bent over, holding her stomach now. I couldn't tell if she was laughing or crying.

"Okay, Katherine, seriously calm down. We still have two years until we have to apply to schools, just let it go." Now Francis was tugging at her arm as she held on to the handle of the door.

"Don't fucking touch me, Francis. You're worthless. You were supposed to make this happen for me and you failed." She gave her arm one powerful tug and her wrist was free again.

Now I was growing impatient. "Listen, I have someone I need to meet. Please move away from the door, Katherine." I said.

"If you didn't tell Kowalski, who did?"

Francis stood in between Katherine and me, "I told her and Angelique."

Now Katherine was practically foaming at the mouth with laughter. "Wow, okay, you really are a snake, Francis. I'll move, but before I do that, I have something I need to get off my chest." Katherine reached into her coach purse and pulled out my letter from Mrs. Johnson that usually hung in my locker in safe keeping.

"Is there anything you won't steal, Katherine?" All the muscles in my body wanted to pounce on her, but when she held the letter up in the air, I noticed a tiny pink lighter moving towards my letter in her other hand.

"Katherine . . ." Francis put up both his hands and moved slowly towards her. "Just stop this, Katherine."

"Of course you'd stick up for her . . ." she said.

Now heat was rising in my chest, and I prepared to lunge at her. But before I could, she lit the letter on fire and tossed it into the large bin basket by the door.

"NO!" I screamed, running towards the bin of trash that was now blazing in flames.

"Are you fucking nuts!" Francis screamed. He body checked her to the ground and held her in place, kicking and screaming. "Em, get some water quickly!"

I ran to the water cooler, but it was empty. Then I remembered my Contigo in my backpack and threw what I could on the fire, but the water wasn't enough to tame the growing flames.

"There's no water!" I screamed, watching Francis pull Katherine away from the door.

"There's a fire extinguisher near the bathroom!" He directed. I ran to the bathroom searching for it, but it wasn't there.

"Do you have a Plan B, Francis?"

Now the fire had spread, and it blocked the exit to the room.

"Francis!" I screamed in panic, but he and Katherine were just staring at the flames in shock. From the photocopier, I spotted a fire alarm and pulled it with all my might. Water stormed over us from the ceiling. Then I picked up an industrial sized hole puncher and used it to shatter one of the large windows.

"We can get out from here!" I screamed.

Francis got up and ran towards the window, helping me get a leg out and pushing me through the window sill of shattered glass. As my feet landed on the grass outside of the building, I watched crowds of students running out of the building to our designated fire route.

After me came Katherine. She was crying hysterically as if she was the victim of this. Then came Francis. He jumped out of the window and landed on his arm.

I looked around me, all eyes were on me. Whispers filled the air and suddenly I knew they would blame me for this. My thoughts were racing and my ears were ringing. I sat with my back against the nearest tree trunk and in an instant adrenaline took over and I blacked out completely.

***

"When the only one you trust betrays you, you have two options to choose from: Forgive the yout, walk away and never look back or bun down d place and watch it burn."

I wrote it in my journal as the female cop came back into the room with an ice cold Ting. Before placing it in front of me, she used her key to take off the metal cap on the opening of the green glass bottle.

"That's some story, Emily." She watched me as I took my first sip of the bubbly grapefruit drink.

"Yea . . . and it's true, officer." I said, hoping she'd believe me.

"Well, your story adds up. We found the pink lighter and evidence of the letter she stole from you. We even have footage of her breaking into your locker, so everything makes sense." She placed her hand on mine as she continued. "Now the question is, will you be pressing charges?"

I closed my eyes; they were stinging from all the crying I had done in the past few hours. "No." I whispered.

The officer asked, "Are you sure, Emily?"

"Yes," I replied.

"Okay then, you are free to go." She said, motioning for my mom to re-enter the room.

I got up from the table and gathered my backpack and journal, getting ready to leave. After a day like this, all I wanted was a bath and some of my grandma's food. I made my way towards the door as my mother waited outside, ready to take me home.

"Emily . . ." the female cop called out, "you're forgetting something." Near the table was a tiny photo that seemed to have fallen out of my bag. She handed it to me. It was the photo of Yvette and her children. The photo she slipped into the envelope she gave me. I flipped it around in my hands and on the back it said, "Thank you sweet girl, whether you feel it or not, you've made a difference in my life."

A tear welled up and rolled down my cheek. "Thanks."

On the drive home, I sat in the front with my mother.

"You okay, baby?" she asked me.

"I think I will be now." I said back.

We drove the rest of the way in silence. I pulled out my phone and sent a text to Michaela, telling her I was out of the police station.

That's awesome girl! You did the right thing.

It felt great having a friend I could tell anything to without worrying about being judged or discouraged. Just as I thought that, we passed Francis' home.

I shook my head and looked away.

"Want some music, my darling?" My mom motioned with her chin towards the radio. I turned up the volume and Toni Braxton's *"He Wasn't Man Enough For Me"* started playing. I looked at my mom and we both laughed.

When we pulled up to the driveway, my grandmother was on the porch walking towards the car. She was wearing a fabulous yellow and green floral maxi dress with a hint of red flowers, topped with a cropped denim jacket. She was also wearing a beautiful pair of sterling silver bar drop earrings that looked very familiar.

"Hey, are you wearing my earrings?" I asked with a laugh.

"Yea, I borrowed them. Can you believe I left all my good jewellery back home?" she laughed.

"Do you want to get something to eat," my mom said, directing her question to all of us.

"Yes, we have some news to celebrate!" I said.

"What news?" my mom said with a shrug.

I was going to drag the suspense out longer, but I was too excited. "A lady from the Toronto Spectator came and offered me a part-time job as a student journalist!" I yelled.

"That's incredible!" my mom screamed, leaning over to me and giving me a hug. "Why didn't you say anything earlier!"

I shrugged.

"Congratulations, my sweet granddaughter," my grandma said, hugging me after.

"Thank you, thank you," I said.

"So where are we going for dinner?" I asked as I motioned for her to join us in the car.

My mom shook her head. With a chuckle, she said to my grandma, "You've spoiled this girl."

"I know, I know," my grandma raised her hand in surrender. Then she laughed and went into the car.

As my mom drove off, I asked, "Okay, but for real, where are we going for dinner? I need to pull up the menu from now so I can decide what I want." I said with a serious face.

My grandma and mom looked at each other and burst out laughing. "Likkle girl, you try put on your seat belt and be quiet," my grandma said through her laughter. My mom bumped some Beres as we drove to God knows where. With my window down, I looked out and allowed the cool breeze to tickle my face.

I peered over at my mother and grandmother as they chatted, laughed, and sang together. I smiled and joined in the festivities. It was complete bliss.

ACKNOWLEDGEMENTS

I've waited a very long time to write my own acknowledgement.
It's surreal.

It may sound cliché but it's necessary. First and foremost, thank you to God for blessing me with the gift of writing. I am grateful that I can use my words to entertain and hopefully educate and motivate readers. It is not a talent that I take lightly.

Mommy, I owe all of this to you. Thank you for buying me my very first journal. Thank you for building a home, where expressing my emotions through writing was embraced. I am grateful for the many storybooks you bought for me. You are the one who enforced reading and comprehension. I remember, as if it were yesterday, the annual summer assignments you would give me; to read a book and then to write what I understood from the book; the themes, the message. Thank you for giving me a voice and for giving me the courage to use it. I am forever indebted to your insurmountable sacrifice.

To my parents-in-law, Cleve and Juliet Russell, thank you for your unconditional support. You two are pillars of strength for me and I love you greatly.

Jada, my only sibling, I know I wrote that Emily is an only child but I did not forget you. Most of the strength that Emily depicts is inspired by you. You are the strongest and wisest teenager I have ever had the pleasure of knowing. You have mastered rejection and hardship with grace. You are self-sufficient and I am so proud of the young woman you are becoming. Akeil, my love, my heart, my biggest headache. You have been my strength in ways that you will never know. I remembered my own strength from observing your ambition, passion and courage for what you do. You are always sure of yourself; always confident and that is one of the traits that I admire the most about you. Thank you for being a huge source of strength. Thank you for being my support system on nights when I was anxious about my writing. Thank you for your patience, but most importantly, thank you for believing in my dream of becoming an author.

Brittany, thank you. Thank you for it all. You are more than just a book coach. Thank you for pushing me to dig deeper with my writing. Thank you for your pure, raw honest feedback. Thank you for inspiring me and making me believe in my writing again. On days when I felt like giving up on publishing this debut novel, you really helped to put things in perspective. I am tremendously grateful to you. Thank you for teaching me how to not only write but to turn my book into a business. Thank you for loving this book as your own.

Dominique, I am eternally grateful for the hard work you have done to bring my vision to life. Since our very first book design meeting, I have been in awe of your work ethic, creativity and your brilliance. Thank you for being a great listener, for taking the time to understand what I wanted for the design of the novel. To be so young in the game and to be killing it is incredibly inspiring. I have no doubt that your career will go even further than you are now.

Thank you to Cristal and Jon for doing amazing jobs as voice actors in the audio excerpt. You both did such a wonderful job of bringing my words to life and evoking emotions across social media.

Natasha, thank you! Thank you for your amazing creativity and brilliance! You exceeded my expectations with the photography and videography that you created. You are extraordinary.

Thank you to all the beta readers who forced me to challenge myself and further develop my plot and characters by providing relevant feedback. A special shoutout to Noria. Girl, you kept me on my toes with your numerous IG DMs. You helped me to maintain my excitement about my book. You have been a strong force of motivation in ways that you will never know. Thank you also to my dearest friends, Racine, Allyson, Jayvonlae, Chadwick and Peter for your never-ending support. I am grateful for every text, call and voice note that checked on the process of my book. I am truly blessed to call you friends.

I possess an immense amount of gratitude to the institutions that have taken a chance on my novel to display it on their shelves, front desk, counters, etc. . . .They include bookstores, libraries, you name it. I am so grateful!

Finally, a special thank you to you, the reader! Your tremendous support does not go unnoticed.

GET YOUR FREE NOVELLA

Shoot Your Shot is a YA coming of age novella about the deeply complex nature of growing up as a teenage woman among violence in Jamaica and the prelude to Julianne Mundle's debut novel, *Come with the Fire*.

Thirteen-year-old Emily Morrison and her best friend, Lexi, live among fragrant citrus trees, towering palm trees, hot sunshine and the deep red dirt roads that lead to the town's most luxurious tropical sanctuary, Alcove Sports Club. Emily seems to have it all: an influential mother who works at the swanky club, a father who wants the best for her, a best friend who is more like a sister, and a chance to ace the GSAT and attend the best high-school in the parish. For the wealthy and influential people on the island, Alcove has always been a spot for gatherings and events . . . outsiders are not allowed. But when members of a yardie gang, from a nearby town, invade the affluent club, a chance encounter leaves Emily traumatized. She's witnessed something she wasn't supposed to see and now she's positive they're coming after her next.

Available Now at cjuliannewrite.com!

www.ingramcontent.com/pod-product-compliance
Lightning Source LLC
Chambersburg PA
CBHW021143190726
48288CB00008B/2796